MONTANA MAVERICKS

Welcome to Big Sky Country! Where spirited men and women discover love on the range.

LEGACY OF TENACITY

As the town begins to heal from its scars and scandals, its single cowboys (and cowgirls) are ready for a fresh start. They know that love can grow in the most unexpected places and that down doesn't mean out. So make a wish on a Montana moon for all to be revealed—they've waited for their sweethearts long enough!

ROPING THE MAVERICK

Everyone says you should bloom where you're planted, but florist Tiffany Brandt can't imagine putting down roots in a place like Tenacity, so far from the city lights. More to the point, she can't picture trusting a man ever again. Rancher Ellis Corey may *seem* like the perfect guy, but she's been fooled before. So while she's in town helping her sister, she's good with being "friends who kiss" with the handsome rancher—until he wants more...

Dear Reader,

One of my favorite tropes is opposites attract. I enjoy watching as two people who could not be more different than each other if they tried find themselves inexplicably attracted to the other. Though they know they are as different as any two people could be, they can't help how they feel. Logic has its strength, but it isn't as strong as the heart. And against two hearts? It doesn't stand a chance.

On the outside, Ellis Corey and Tiffany Brandt have nothing in common. He loves the wide-open spaces of his ranch and she loves the hustle and bustle of the city. She enjoys spa days and shopping at fancy boutiques for fashionable clothes. He's happy in old jeans. And a facial or professional manicure? Forget about it. Yet despite their brains telling them they're too different to ever be happy together, they can't stay apart. Who knows, maybe by spending more time together, they'll discover that they aren't all that different. At least in the ways that matter.

I hope you enjoy reading *Roping the Maverick* as much as I enjoyed writing it.

For more information about my other Montana Mavericks or Special Edition books, visit my website, kathydouglassbooks.com. While you're there, sign up for my newsletter or drop me a note. I love hearing from my readers.

Happy reading!

Kathy

ROPING THE MAVERICK

KATHY DOUGLASS

Special thanks and acknowledgment are given to Kathy Douglass for her contribution to the Montana Mavericks: Legacy of Tenacity miniseries.

Recycling programs for this product may not exist in your area.

ISBN-13: 978-1-335-54089-8

Roping the Maverick

Harlequin Enterprises ULC
22 Adelaide St. West, 41st Floor
Toronto, Ontario M5H 4E3, Canada
www.Harlequin.com

HarperCollins Publishers
Macken House, 39/40 Mayor Street Upper,
Dublin 1, D01 C9W8, Ireland
www.HarperCollins.com

Printed in Lithuania

Kathy Douglass is a lawyer turned author of sweet small-town contemporary romances. She is married to her very own hero and mother to two sons, who cheer her on as she tries to get her stubborn hero and heroine to realize they are meant to be together. She loves hearing from readers that something in her books made them laugh or cry. You can learn more about Kathy or contact her at kathydouglassbooks.com.

Books by Kathy Douglass

Montana Mavericks: Legacy of Tenacity

Roping the Maverick

Montana Mavericks: The Trail to Tenacity

That Maverick of Mine

Montana Mavericks: The Anniversary Gift

Starting Over with the Maverick

Harlequin Special Edition

Aspen Creek Bachelors

Valentines for the Rancher
The Rancher's Baby
Wrangling a Family
The Cowboy Who Came Home
A Reunion to Remember

Visit the Author Profile page
at Harlequin.com for more titles.

This book is dedicated with love and appreciation
to my husband and sons. Thank you for
always believing in me and supporting me
as I pursue my dreams. I couldn't do this without you.

Chapter One

Tiffany Brandt looked out her hotel room to the small eastern Montana town. There really wasn't much to see. *I'm not in Bronco anymore.* Though Tenacity was only an hour and a half away from her hometown of Bronco, it may as well be on another planet. Sure, parts of Bronco were working class—her parents had raised Tiffany and her siblings on that side of town—but it was significantly better off than this town.

Tenacity was a hardscrabble, blue-collar town made up mostly of ranchers. From what she'd been able to observe, the people were barely scraping by. Tenacity was definitely in thc bcfore stage of the hoped for renaissance. The dining options were limited to say the least. The Silver Spur Café served breakfast and lunch and Castillo's Mexican Restaurant was good for dinner. There wasn't a high-class dining establishment in sight. And forget about shopping for clothes or shoes. You could count the businesses on one hand and still have fingers left over. It wasn't the type of place Tiffany would choose to visit, and she would miss stopping in at Bronco Java and Juice for her afternoon pick-me-up.

But her sister Stephanie needed her. And sisters helped each other.

"Stop frowning before your face freezes that way."

Tiffany laughed and then flashed her sister an exaggerated smile. Stephanie was holding her sweet baby girl in her arms, bouncing her up and down. At ten months old, Melanie didn't like the restriction of being held, and she strained against her mother. Sighing, Stephanie set the baby onto the floor and then stood. Melanie grabbed on to the faded blue and silver spread on the queen-size bed and then dropped onto her diapered bottom.

"I was just looking at the town." Such as it was.

"And no doubt mourning the fact that there is not a spa as far as the eye can see. I don't know how you'll manage without a hot stone massage." Stephanie's voice held more than a hint of humor. All three of the Brandt sisters appreciated the finer things in life, but where Brittany and Stephanie considered them wants, Tiffany thought of them as needs.

"I work hard and I like to pamper myself occasionally. Is that a crime?"

"Not at all," Stephanie said quickly. "This is a no judgment zone. And just to show my appreciation for your sacrifice in coming to Tenacity to help me, when we get back home, I'm going to arrange a sister day at the spa. You, me and Brittany. The whole works. My treat."

"Now you're singing my song. But it really isn't necessary for you to pay. You know that I love Melanie. Watching her while you help Geoff with his rodeo commitments will be my pleasure. And it will solidify my position as Melanie's favorite aunt."

Stephanie's husband, Geoff Burris, was the biggest star in rodeo and had held that position for years. Geoff and Stephanie met when he was injured during a photo shoot at the Bronco Convention Center and was taken to the hospital where Stephanie worked as a nurse. It didn't take long for them to fall in love. Now he was lending his name and expertise to Tenacity's inaugural rodeo that would coincide with their Dinosaur Days festival—something that Tiffany wanted to learn more about.

"This is going to be such a busy and chaotic time. I like knowing that Melanie will be in good hands."

Tiffany held up her perfectly manicured hands and grinned. "The best."

"You know, Mayor Garrett and the town leaders are trying to attract new businesses to this town. You can always open a second Tiffany in Bloom flower shop here. Geoff and I can mention your shop when we meet with them. You're so successful that you should think about opening a second location."

Tiffany in Bloom was more than just a place to buy a dozen red roses on Valentine's Day. She offered classes where she taught students how to make lovely arrangements on any budget. She also provided gardening tips, helping her students select the best flowers and shrubs to maximize the appearance of their landscaping. When you walked out of her class, you knew everything from how to select the perfect vase to knowing which types of plants to choose for your sun and shade balance. Tiffany liked knowing that she was doing her part to make the world a more beautiful place. But she didn't know if she had the skill to work that kind of magic here. Tenacity needed more than even Tiffany had the ability to provide.

Tiffany looked at her sister, not sure whether Stephanie was serious or not, but she decided to treat the question as if she was.

"The thought has crossed my mind lately—opening a second location, not opening one here in Tenacity," Tiffany hastened to clarify. "I doubt a florist would be able to break even here. Besides, until I'm certain that opening a second location is something that I want to do—something I have time to do—I'll have to make do with my Blossom Truck. I'm able to travel to outdoor festivals and farmers markets, reaching customers who are unable to come to my shop."

Stephanie shook her head. "I can't believe my fashionable sister likes driving around in a van looking like something from the 1960s."

"People love my Blossom Truck. Especially kids, who by the way know nothing about flower power. Heck, I didn't know anything about it myself until Mom and Dad told me about it."

Stephanie gave Tiffany a serious look. "How are you really? I know this isn't exactly what you were expecting."

She swept out her arm. Her gesture encompassed the entire room. There wasn't a Jacuzzi tub or California king in sight. Nor did the room come with plush robes and slippers for her comfort or a personalized welcome gift. But the Tenacity Inn was clean and the people she'd interacted with were kind and knowledgeable. So she would have to manage without twenty-four hour room service for the duration of her stay.

"What makes you say that?"

"I saw the clothes that you brought with you."

Though she would only be in town for a short time, Tiffany had packed a variety of outfits. She liked to be prepared for every eventuality. She thought of the fancy dress and designer clothes hanging in the small closet. Most of them would be repacked in her suitcase without being worn. Tenacity was a faded jeans and T-shirt kind of town.

Three good things, Tiffany reminded herself. Every night, before she went to bed, she made herself think of three good things that had happened to her during the day. It was going to take supreme effort to find even one good thing if she let negativity take hold, so she swept it away.

Tiffany had started the practice several years ago after a relationship ended disastrously. Discovering that her former fiancé had been deceiving her had broken more than her heart. It had wounded her pride and nearly crushed her spirit. Something inside her had shifted and she'd begun to look at the world, and the people in it, in a negative light. When she realized that she was becoming a bitter and mean person that even she didn't like, Tiffany knew that she'd needed an attitude adjustment. So she'd begun to look for things to be grateful for. It had helped to a degree. She was once again a positive person. But positive thinking couldn't fix everything. Even now, years later, she was still wary of risking her heart and she avoided serious relationships at all costs.

"I'm fine. It will be an adventure."

Stephanie didn't look convinced, but before she could say anything further, her phone beeped. She looked at the screen and smiled as she read her text. Then her smile faded and she looked at Tiffany, concern in her eyes. "That was Geoff. Apparently he needs me for an impromptu interview. I know you hadn't planned on watching Melanie right now, but do you mind?"

"Of course I don't mind," Tiffany said. "That's why I'm here. If you get her stroller, I'll take her for a walk around town. We can explore Tenacity together."

"You're a lifesaver," Stephanie said before darting out of the room. In a minute she was back, pushing the stroller. She shoved a diaper bag into the basket under the seat, picked up Melanie and kissed her cheek, then handed the little girl to Tiffany. "See you later, sweetie."

Tiffany smiled as she watched her sister leave. Then she looked back at her niece. "What do you think about a spin around town, Miss Melanie?"

The baby chortled and placed her hands on Tiffany's cheeks and then patted them.

"I'll take that as a yes." After checking the baby's diaper, Tiffany settled her into the stroller, draped her crossbody purse over her torso and headed for the elevator. The Tenacity Inn was small, only four floors, but on the whole it was serviceable. Tiffany thought that she would have placed vibrant floral arrangements in the lobby as she pushed the stroller through the unadorned space. But since they were the only game in town, they might not feel the need to go the extra mile. Or they could be struggling like she'd been told some other businesses in town were.

Once she was standing on the sidewalk, Tiffany looked left and then right, trying to decide which way to go. Since she was unfamiliar with the town and didn't have any particular destination in mind, she decided to go right. Though the buildings she passed were not particularly new, the streets had been swept clean of trash. As always, she looked at the area with a florist's eye. With proper landscaping, some colorful flowerbeds, decorative lighting and a few strategically placed benches, the town would feel cheerier.

She walked another block, passing two people who nodded. She returned the gesture and continued on her way. She couldn't help but compare Tenacity to Bronco Heights. Though she hadn't mentioned it to Stephanie, she missed BH Couture dress shop where she would pop in just to see what they had. The same with Beaumont and Rossi's Fine Jewels. And she was a regular at Coeur de l'Ouest restaurant. Knowing she wouldn't be visiting her regular haunts was disappointing.

Perhaps she should think of three good things now instead of waiting. She took a deep breath. *One.* The sky was a beautiful clear blue. *Two.* The weather was perfect. Just the temperature she would have ordered if she could. *Three.* She was spending time with her sweet niece. Life couldn't get much better than that.

Once more feeling positive, she was smiling as she came upon a park. Leaves were budding on the trees and there were patches of green in the grass. Tiffany saw a flyer advertising the upcoming dinosaur dig. The notion that dinosaur bones were buried here was fascinating and she wanted to know more about it. Sadly, the flyer didn't contain many details.

"I guess I'll just have to make up a story on my own. How does that sound, Melanie? Do you want me to tell you about the dinosaur dig? It won't be true, but I guarantee it will be entertaining."

Melanie gurgled and kicked her chubby legs.

"I hope you don't mind if I listen, too."

Tiffany turned at the sound of the amused voice. It was deep and intriguing and incredibly sexy. When she looked into the face of the man who'd spoken, Tiffany realized that the voice fit him. With brown eyes, high cheekbones and a sculpted nose and chin, he was sexiness personified. Tiffany's heart skipped a ridiculous beat.

"I don't know," she said, unable to keep from returning the man's smile. "For all I know, you're a literary critic, waiting to tear my story apart. I don't think my fragile ego can take it."

He laughed and a shiver danced down her spine. What in the world was going on? She had sworn off men. Especially handsome men oozing charm. "I'm nothing of the sort. I'm a simple rancher. My family and I own a spread outside of town."

"Oh," she said. "So you're a local?"

"Yes." He extended a hand. "Ellis Corey."

She shook his hand. It was warm and she liked the way her hand felt in his. "Tiffany Brandt."

"Nice to meet you, Tiffany."

"Same. So you probably know about the upcoming dinosaur dig."

"I do indeed. You can't live in Tenacity and not know about it. Ask me anything."

She laughed. "I want to know everything. Are dinosaur bones really buried here or is it a gimmick to draw attention to this town?"

"Oh, it's not a gimmick. There are dinosaur bones buried in Tenacity."

"What makes people think that? Maybe it's just a rumor. You know, like crop circles and aliens."

He smiled and dimples flashed in his cheeks. "Ah. You're a skeptic."

"Not really. I just have questions." She looked at him, one eyebrow raised. "Questions that you said you would answer."

"So I did. We've already found some dinosaur bones, and now we're hoping to find more with this dig. The dig will start in a few weeks when the ground is softer. Then we'll hopefully find more bones. Maybe even a complete dinosaur." He held up his hands, fingers crossed. "This will be a good thing for the town. Tenacity can use something to drum up interest in our little corner of the world. A dinosaur skeleton will definitely do the trick. That's why we're making such a big deal about it. We're having a big festival. Dinosaur Days will bring in lots of visitors to enjoy the events. There's even going to be a rodeo."

Tiffany laughed. "We know all about that, don't we, Melanie? Your daddy is going to be starring in it."

"Her daddy?"

"Yes. Geoff Burris. I don't know if you're into rodeo or not, but he's very popular on the circuit."

"I'm a huge rodeo fan. But even if I wasn't I'd still recognize the name. Geoff Burris is world-famous."

"That's why I'm here in Tenacity. He's helping the organizers with the details. He's also doing publicity with press and TV networks from around the country to increase interest in the rodeo and, by extension, Dinosaur Days. Everyone wants a piece of him. I'm sure every businesses in Tenacity wants a photo with Geoff to hang on their walls."

"That must get tiring for you. I can see why you and your daughter took a break to come to the park."

Tiffany laughed. "You think I'm Geoff's wife?"

"You said she was his daughter. And the family resemblance between the two of you is unmistakable."

"That's because I'm her aunt. Geoff is married to my sister, Stephanie. Stephanie is a private person by nature, but she agreed to do a few photo shoots and interviews with Geoff. But she insisted that their daughter not be included in any media events. She wants Melanie to grow up out of the limelight. When she's old enough, she can decide for herself if she wants a more public life."

"That makes sense."

"I have my own business in Bronco Heights. I'm getting some renovations done on the building at the moment that prevent me from being open, so when Geoff and Stephanie asked me to come along to help with my niece, I agreed. I love spoiling this little angel."

Ellis glanced at Tiffany's left hand and his smile

broadened. He'd been friendly before, but now his smile held a hint of flirtation and a double dose of charm. Tiffany knew that she should be wary, but there was something about him that piqued her interest. Besides, what did it matter if they flirted? Nothing would come of it. She would see to that. There was absolutely no way she would even consider getting involved with another man, especially this one. Given that he was at least a second-generation rancher, his roots ran deep. She couldn't imagine him picking up stakes to follow her back to Bronco. Not that she wanted him to.

"Since you aren't married to Geoff Burris, are you married to anyone?"

"No."

"In that case, would you like to go out with me?"

She gave him a pointed look. "Just because I'm not married doesn't mean I'm not in a relationship. I could have a boyfriend."

"Fair enough. Is there anyone you need to break up with so you can go out with me?"

Tiffany couldn't hold back a laugh. "Pretty sure of yourself, aren't you?"

"Not at all. I just don't want to step on anyone's toes."

"Not to worry. I'm not seeing anyone."

"So, does that mean you'll go out with me?"

She knew there had to be at least a dozen good reasons to say no, but suddenly none of them were persuasive enough for her to reject him. "Where would we go?"

"What do you mean *where would we go*?"

"Don't get me wrong, I'm sure the people in this

town are lovely, but I haven't seen any place that is date-worthy. If you know what I mean."

"I know exactly what you mean." His eyes traveled over her body, taking in her stylish slacks and blouse in a quick glance that left her feeling breathless. "You aren't the cowboy-boot-wearing, hang-out-at-a-saloon type of girl."

"Exactly. I don't want to insult you or your town, but to be honest, I don't exactly fit in here."

"I'm not the least bit offended. People are free to like what they like."

Tiffany smiled. He was so charming. So easygoing. So *sexy*. The idea of spending more time with him—even in a non-date-worthy place—was more appealing than she wanted to admit. Then she glanced at Melanie and sighed. "I can't. I told Stephanie and Geoff they could count on me to watch Melanie whenever they needed. I don't know when I'll be free. I don't want to make a promise to you that I won't be able to keep."

"That's not a problem. You can bring the baby with you."

"You want to take a ten-month-old on a date?"

He shrugged, and Tiffany was momentarily distracted by the movement of his massive shoulders beneath his cotton shirt. She'd never been attracted to overly muscular men before. In her experience, the more developed the muscles, the less developed the brain and empathy. But despite Ellis's physique, he seemed both smart and caring. "Why not?"

Why not indeed? "Okay. Then yes."

"Great. We'll have a good time."

"Where will this fun date with a kid take place? I've only been in town for a day, but that was long enough for me to discover that entertainment options are limited."

"How about we meet right here in the park the day after tomorrow? We're enjoying a stretch of good weather so we may as well take advantage of it. I'll bring lunch and a blanket and we can let your niece play."

"That does sound nice." For all of her love of luxuries, Tiffany liked simple things, too. She absolutely loved spending time in nature. Especially in the spring, which was her favorite season. "What can I bring?"

"Yourself. I invited you."

"Still, I'll feel funny showing up empty-handed."

"Why? If we were going to a restaurant, you wouldn't bring anything. At least I don't think you would pull a pie out of your purse. Since we've just met, I guess I shouldn't make that assumption."

Tiffany shook her head as she laughed. "You are so silly."

"But am I wrong?"

"No. You're right. I wouldn't bring a pie, but I might insist on paying for my own meal. Which is along the same lines of me bringing something."

"You aren't going to make this easy for me, are you?"

"Is there a reason why I should?" she teased.

A dimple flashed in his cheek. "Because I'm a nice guy?"

She laughed. "I think you've gotten about all the mileage you can from your charm. At least for today."

"Okay. But unless you plan on packing your own lunch and each of us having a separate dining experience, I'll bring the food and you can supply the stimulating conversation."

"If you insist."

"I do. So is it a date?"

"It's a date."

Ellis blew out a breath. He hadn't worked this hard to get a woman to go out on a date with him in…well, ever. He'd always had a way with the ladies. He couldn't recall a time when he hadn't been popular. Women had always liked spending time with him and he'd never wanted for female companionship.

Ellis knew he'd led a charmed life. He was from a good family that loved each other unconditionally. Both sets of grandparents were healthy and doing well, although his maternal grandparents had retired to Hilton Head, South Carolina, several years ago and were living the good life. His paternal grandparents were well respected here in town. The same could be said for his parents, aunts and uncles. Ellis had the best siblings and cousins anyone could ask for. All in all, he knew that when it came to family he had it better than most.

Once he'd thought his good fortune was unending. The results of the Tenacity mayoral election a few months ago had disabused him of that notion. The field of candidates had been crowded, but he'd actually believed that he would come out on top. There had been some election tampering that had broken his heart as much as it had angered him. The idea that someone in

Tenacity would cheat in order to get into power had been unthinkable. People in other places might put their own selfish ambition ahead of fair play, but in Tenacity? He'd thought they were better than that.

But his hurt couldn't compare to that of JenniLynn Garrett. Her husband had actually colluded with one of the other candidates in order to ensure that she didn't win. Once the tampering had been discovered, she had been declared the winner. Though it was an undisputable fact that she was doing a good job as mayor, it did little to soothe his bruised ego and hurt feelings. He'd been sure he was going to be mayor and had planned his life around doing that job. Now he was at loose ends and was trying to figure out his next move.

After the election, he'd briefly considered leaving town and starting over fresh somewhere else. That notion hadn't lasted long. Tenacity was his home and his roots were sunk deep here. Six generations of Coreys had been ranchers here through good times and bad. They'd contributed to the town and he intended to make his mark as well. Tenacity was in the before stage of the long-awaited renaissance, but the *after* was in sight. The town's fortunes were improving and, mayor or not, he was going to do his part to see that things kept moving in the right direction.

Ellis and Tiffany exchanged numbers and then he left her to play with her niece. He'd been on his way to the Strom and Son Feed and Farm Supply store when he'd first spotted her walking down the street. There was something about her that had attracted him and he'd stopped and stared. Dressed in a pair of yellow slacks, a pink and yellow blouse and a yellow jacket, she'd looked like a ray of sunshine. His trip to the feed store had quickly lost prominence in his mind, replaced by the need to meet this beautiful stranger. The more they'd talked, the more attracted he'd become. She would have been perfect if not for the fact that she was only in town for a short while. And since she owned her own business in Bronco, she more than likely wouldn't be able to extend her stay.

Not only that, he'd seen the look on her face when she'd glanced around town. Very little, if anything had appealed to her. Her words might have been spoken kindly, but he'd heard her loud and clear. She didn't like the town that he loved. When the rodeo was over, she would be packing her bags and leaving town, never to return. That was fine with him. He wasn't looking for a relationship. He needed to figure out his next step before he invited a woman into his life. And that woman wouldn't turn her nose up at his town.

But there was nothing stopping him from enjoying her company.

Chapter Two

"Don't you look nice?"

"Thanks." Though Tiffany didn't think anything could come of her date with Ellis, she'd put on her favorite blue-and-green blouse and green slacks. She'd styled her hair simply, letting the curls tumble over her shoulders. Her makeup was subtle yet impeccable. Tiffany didn't believe in doing anything halfway and would never leave the house looking anything other than her best. She turned to her sister. "Do you think it's too much? It's only lunch in the park after all."

Stephanie shook her head. "Of course not. It's still a date, isn't it?"

"I wouldn't call it a date, exactly. More like two people meeting for lunch. After all, Ellis was open to including Melanie. I can still bring her with me if necessary."

"First, what you described is the very definition of a date. You and Ellis having a secluded lunch in the park. It has a hint of romance in it," Stephanie teased.

Tiffany crossed her arms across her chest and leaned her hip against the arm of the chair. "I wouldn't go that far."

"Second," Stephanie continued as if Tiffany hadn't spoken, "there is no need for you to bring Melanie. I won't be doing press with Geoff today. He's got meetings with the rodeo organizers, so Melanie and I will be spending the day together. But I'll make sure that we avoid the park. We don't want to intrude on what may be the beginning of a beautiful relationship."

"Not every date leads to a relationship, beautiful or otherwise."

"So, you agree that this is a date," Stephanie said, a triumphant grin on her face.

Tiffany blew out an exasperated breath. "You're really sneaky, you know that?"

Stephanie laughed. "Whatever it takes to get you to see the light."

"Whatever. But you never answered my question. Do you think I'm overdressed?"

"No. You look perfect."

"Then I guess I should get on the road." She picked up a bouquet of flowers that she'd created for Ellis from several bundles of flowers she'd bought at Tenacity Grocery. Some of them had seen better days, but she'd coaxed the best of them into a bouquet worthy of her name.

"Have a great time," Stephanie said.

"That's the plan." Tiffany blew her sister a kiss, then headed out the door. Ellis had offered to pick her up, but she'd told him she would rather meet him. Tiffany hadn't known if Stephanie and Geoff would be around and she wasn't ready for the whole meet-the-family thing. It just made things seem so official. Besides, there was no guarantee that she and Ellis would even like each other, which made those introductions unnecessary at this point.

The warm and sunny day was perfect for an alfresco lunch. Two birds flew overhead and Tiffany watched them fly until they were out of sight. When she reached the park, Ellis was already there, leaning against a shiny red pickup with a blue-and-white patchwork quilt draped over a cooler near his feet. Dressed in a blue shirt that hugged his broad shoulders and chest and faded jeans that emphasized his muscular thighs, he looked good enough to almost make Tiffany forget that she wasn't looking for a relationship. *Almost.* Her heart had been shredded once before and she wasn't willing to take that step again simply because a man possessed the body of a Greek god. Besides, she had a thriving business in Bronco that she had built from the ground up. She was paying good money to have the building renovated. It didn't make sense for her to become emotionally attached to someone who lived in another town.

But that didn't mean that she couldn't enjoy the view and do a bit of harmless flirting.

When Ellis spotted her, he pushed away from the truck and walked in her direction. When his eyes landed on the bouquet she'd created for him, he smiled. "What's this?" His voice rang with surprise and pleasure.

"It's a bouquet. Why? What's it look like?"

"Funny."

"It looks funny?" Tiffany placed a hand on her hip and then glanced at Ellis, a grin on her face. "I'll have you know that I am a highly skilled florist. Tiffany in Bloom is one of the most successful businesses in Bronco Heights. I create spectacular floral arrangements that are second to none. People come from miles around just to purchase my bouquets. I assure you that there is nothing funny about these flowers."

Ellis laughed. It was a robust sound that sent a dangerous shiver down her spine. "I meant that you were… amusing. The flowers are nice. But I don't understand. Why are you giving them to me?"

"Flowers might be my business, but I enjoy receiving a bouquet every now and then. Most people do. I figured you might like them. Was I wrong?"

"No. I like them. It's just that nobody else has ever given me flowers before."

"That's because no one else is like me."

"You are definitely one of a kind, Tiffany Brandt."

She handed him the bouquet. He looked so happy that she was tempted to pull out her phone so she could capture this moment. She shooed the thought away. This lunch wasn't the beginning of a serious relationship, so there was no need to document anything. She was only here for a good time. "Surely you're not just noticing that."

"No. I noticed the minute I saw you walking down the street. That's when I knew I had to get to know you."

His charm was definitely lethal. Though she wanted to believe he was simply flirting with her, that this was just a well-worn line that he used on all the women he met, the sincerity in his voice cast some doubt on that theory and her heart fluttered. A more cautious woman would have made an excuse and walked away. But no one had ever accused Tiffany of being cautious. Reckless was a more apt descriptor.

"You are quite the charmer."

"I was hoping you would notice."

It was impossible not to notice. It was also impossible to resist. She looked around. There were a few picnic benches under a wooden canopy not too far away. A few crows were on the tables, but otherwise the area was empty. "Where do you want to sit?"

"I thought we could walk around a bit first. The food should keep for a while longer."

"That sounds like a plan. Lead the way."

Ellis held out his hand and Tiffany took it without hesitation. His palm was calloused, a sign that he did physical labor. Of course she didn't need that additional proof. His muscular body was evidence enough.

"I thought we might head over to the site of the dinosaur dig. We might not be able to get close to it when Dinosaur Days begin. At least not if the crowds are as big as I'm hoping they'll be."

"You mentioned the dinosaur bones the other day. Can you tell me more about them?"

"Sure. There were some archeologists here not long ago. They found bones and believe there are more. Don't ask me to be more specific because I can't. I'm a rancher, not a scientist."

"So this is like a dinosaur cemetery."

"I wouldn't go that far. I don't know how many dinosaurs they believe are buried here."

"And the powers that be think it's a good idea to unbury them? Didn't any of you people see the *Jurassic Park* movies?"

"Nobody is trying to create new dinosaurs from DNA. I agree that would be problematic."

"So why dig up the bones? Why disturb their final resting place instead of letting them rest in peace?"

"A couple of reasons. First, this is an important scientific discovery. This is a way to learn more about dinosaurs and what happened to them. It's a way to learn more about the history of the earth."

"I concede that knowledge is a good thing."

"Second, if there are more dinosaur bones buried here, it could be a boon for Tenacity. Right now the town is struggling and people are tightening their belts. You can see that for yourself. There are few job opportunities so young people graduate high school and move away in search of a well-paying job. There is nothing here to attract tourists. We get the occasional motorist who stops in for a sandwich at the diner before hitting the road again. Then there are people like you and your sister's family who stay at The Tenacity Inn for a few days. But for the most part, people don't visit Tenacity. They pass through on their way to someplace else. If we had some attraction, people might be inclined to make Tenacity their destination. The town could support more businesses and young people wouldn't have to leave town and their families in order to find work."

"And you think these dinosaur bones could be it."

"Without a doubt. I did a little research when talk about the dinosaur bones being buried here began to circulate. The Field Museum of Natural History in Chicago has an almost complete dinosaur. When Sue—that's the dinosaur's name—was first brought to the museum, they saw almost ten thousand visitors within ten hours. That was up from four thousand visitors the same day of the previous week."

"Surely you aren't equating Tenacity to Chicago." She didn't want to insult his town, but really… "There's no comparison."

"I know that. I was simply making the point that if we had such an attraction, we would get more tourists. Tenacity could go from a sleepy little town to a place that people would choose to vacation. We don't need millions of visitors. We can't handle millions. But thousands would be welcome."

"I hope it works out for you."

"It will."

They walked until they came upon a sunny space in the middle of the park. A few crocuses poked up out of the ground. The trees were beginning to bud and early spring flowers were making their debut. Tiffany could imagine just how beautiful the park would be in the coming months when the trees were filled with leaves, the grass was green and the flowers were in full bloom. She was almost sorry she wouldn't be here to see it. She turned to Ellis. "This is lovely. How about we eat here?"

"Sounds good to me."

Ellis spread the quilt on the ground, set the cooler on it and gestured for Tiffany to sit down. Ellis opened the cooler and began to unload it. As the number of containers grew, Tiffany smiled. "Just how deep is that cooler? It's like a circus clown car. Instead of clowns there are covered bowls."

"It's magic."

Tiffany picked up two containers and sighed. "There's so much good food to choose from."

"I bet you didn't think that you could find variety in Tenacity, did you?"

"No," Tiffany said, not bothering to deny it. "I've been in town for a couple of days and the dining options have been limited to say the least. There isn't a restaurant at the inn so we either have the Silver Spur Cafe or Castillo's. Don't get me wrong, the food at Castillo's is delicious. And the service is great. But I'm used to having more restaurants to choose from."

"Well, it sounds as if you're missing a couple of places."

After filling her plate with a little bit of everything, Tiffany took a bite of a rib. "Oh. These are delicious. I didn't think you could get ribs anywhere in town, much less ones that taste this good."

"Obviously you haven't been to The Grizzly Bar."

Tiffany laughed. "No. I can honestly say I haven't been there. Is that where you got the ribs?"

"Yep."

"Do you go there a lot?"

"Sure. But not just for food. It's a gathering spot. I go there when I want to shoot pool or to hang out with friends. It's laid-back, you know? It's more of a saloon than a restaurant though."

That fit Tiffany's image of the town. More downtown than uptown. But the ribs were tasty. Almost as good as DJ's Deluxe back home in Bronco. Maybe they could go there in the future. She forced the ridiculous thought from her mind and focused on the current conversation. "What's it like?"

"Picture a place with wooden floors, a jukebox and long bar. Oh, and there's an antler chandelier."

"That sounds…interesting."

"Spoken like a true big city girl."

"Bronco isn't exactly a big city. But it does have a lot of the amenities that big cities have."

"If the dinosaur thing pans out the way I hope it will, Tenacity will also have some of those amenities."

"Maybe. But that will still take time. Successful businesses don't just spring up overnight. They're not flowers that can get by with just water and sunshine."

"True. But you have to start somewhere. The Dinosaurs Days festival is just the beginning. Just about every person in town is working hard to make it a success. From the oldest to the youngest. Everyone is contributing in some way. Even the preschool kids are involved."

"Three year olds? Now you're exaggerating."

"No, I'm not." He took a swallow of his soda before continuing. "My grandmother is the co-owner of the Little Cowpokes Daycare Center. She has her little ones participating. You know how irresistible preschoolers are. We have to take advantage of all that cuteness. And then there's the rodeo. You probably know better than most how popular Geoff Burris is. Fans from all over will be flocking to town for the opportunity to see him compete. Not to mention that my brother's future wife and her sisters and cousins will be competing, too."

Tiffany paused, her fork of potato salad suspended inches from her lips. "Wait a minute. Is your brother engaged to one of the Hawkins Sisters?"

"Yes. Remi Hawkins. Do you know her?"

"I do, although I haven't seen her in a while. We're not exactly related but we're part of the same extended family. Two of her sisters are married to Geoff's brothers. We tend to run into each other when the entire family gets together. She's a sweet person. Your brother is a lucky guy."

"So he tells me over and over. Especially when he's trying to convince me that I should take the plunge." Ellis shook his head, clearly exasperated.

"What is it with married people? Ever since Stephanie and my other sister, Brittany, got married, they've developed this single-minded focus to find me a man. It's like they can't rest until I'm married or at least one half of a happy couple. I keep telling them that I'm perfectly happy being single, but they don't want to accept that."

"It's ridiculous. Especially since before Shane met Remi he was happily single."

"Same with my sisters. They have extremely short memories."

Tiffany and Ellis shared smiles. It was good to know that they were on the same page when it came to relationships. Nothing was more awkward than when one person wanted forever and the other person was simply looking to enjoy the moment.

"Well, I'm glad that we understand each other," Ellis said. "This is simply a here-and-now thing."

"Exactly."

Tiffany was glad that they were in agreement and that they could skip the uncomfortable period of not knowing what the other person was thinking or hoping for. She could relax and not worry that Ellis might misconstrue something she said as a desire for a relationship.

Ellis and Tiffany laughed and talked as they ate and the conversation never lapsed. Tiffany was surprised to discover that although their lives were vastly different, they shared the same values. They each valued family and community as well as honesty and loyalty.

"I really enjoyed myself," Tiffany said as they stacked the dishes and containers in the cooler.

Ellis shook the crumbs from the quilt and expertly folded it. Then he flashed her a wide smile. "You sound surprised, as if you didn't expect to."

"I'm not surprised that I had fun," she clarified. "I'm just surprised by how much fun I had. There's a difference."

"Either way, I'm glad that you had a good time. That was my plan," he said as they strolled back across the park. When they reached his truck, he put the cooler and blanket into the back seat and he looked at her. "If you want, I can drive you back to the inn."

"That's not necessary. It's a lovely day and the inn isn't far. I'll walk."

"If you don't mind, then, I'll walk with you."

"I'd like that."

"I still can't get over the fact that you gave me flowers," Ellis said. He took one of the blooms from the bouquet that Tiffany had given him and poked the stem through the top buttonhole on his shirt. He looked quite debonair. After placing the bouquet onto the driver's seat, he closed the truck door, then locked it with the key fob.

"Every person should be surrounded by beauty."

He glanced at her, his gaze warm. "I am."

There he went again, flirting with her. Despite knowing that he was simply being charming, something she believed was second nature for him, her stomach fluttered. Ever since Clive had broken her heart, she'd maintained strict control over her emotions. She never let herself come close to feeling…well, anything. She hadn't even allowed herself to joke around with other men. And flirting had been out of the question. Now she couldn't seem to stop herself. Nor did she want to.

Tiffany hadn't been on more than a handful of dates since that relationship ended, and none in the past year. None of the men she'd dated had rated a second date. Truth be told, she'd been anxious for the first dates to come to an end. Not so today. She supposed the fact that she'd been willing to meet Ellis for lunch and to spend even more time with him now was a sign that she was on her way to healing. Of course, going on one date was a long way from being willing to risk her heart again. But since neither of them wanted a relationship, there wasn't much risk involved.

The park wasn't far from the inn and in under ten minutes, they were standing in the deserted lobby. Ellis looked at her, his full lips curved into a devilish smile. Suddenly the large lobby felt small. Intimate. “I’ll say goodbye here.”

Tiffany nodded. Ellis took a step closer to her and she inhaled, getting a whiff of his masculine scent. The smell of fresh air lingered on his clothes. Being this close to him sent every thought flying from her mind, leaving her a jumble of emotions. Time stood still while Ellis slowly leaned down and brushed his lips against hers. They were warm and the pressure was gentle. He raised his head and looked into her eyes, a question in his. Without giving herself time to reconsider, Tiffany raised herself up on her tiptoes, wrapped her hands around his neck and pulled his head back down to hers for one more kiss.

After a few pleasurable moments, they broke away. Wondering where her good sense had gone to hide, Tiffany looked around the lobby. It was still as empty as before. Thank goodness. Though she was an adult and not doing anything wrong, she understood that her behavior had an impact on her family, including Geoff. She knew how easily things could get blown out of proportion. An innocent kiss could be turned into something else the more times the story was told. That was how gossip took hold and reputations were tarnished—if not ruined.

“Well,” Ellis said, a slight smile on his lips, clearly unbothered about gossip. Tiffany wondered if he ever frowned. He seemed so content all of the time, as if nothing ever got to him. “That was some kiss.”

“Yeah. Well, don’t get any ideas,” Tiffany said as

much to herself as to him. “We’re only going to be friends.”

“Friends who kiss?”

Ellis’s voice was so hopeful and his expression so mischievous that Tiffany couldn’t hold back a laugh. “I suppose so. If the time is right.”

“To me, the time is always right.”

“Figures you’d think that way. Men usually do. But it doesn’t work that way.”

“How does it work? How will I know if the time is right?”

“I’ll let you know.”

“Will we have a signal? You know, like waving your hand in the air? Or perhaps something more subtle. Like clearing your throat.”

“You know, you’re really silly,” Tiffany said, laughing again.

“I don’t want to miss my opportunity.”

“I wouldn’t worry about that if I were you.” She patted his chest. It was even harder than it looked.

“Was that it?” Ellis asked, his eyes dancing with amusement.

“No. That was me signaling that I’m going to my room. I’ll talk to you later.” Though she wanted one more kiss, Tiffany forced herself to walk away from him. Kissing him felt so good that she could easily become addicted. That would only lead to trouble. And she’d had enough of that kind of trouble to last a lifetime. Her back may have been to him, but she felt Ellis’s eyes on her. She knew that he didn’t leave the lobby until the elevator doors had closed behind her. Tiffany pressed the button for her floor and then leaned against the wall. Whew. One thing was true. *Ellis Corey was one heck of a kisser.*

Just thinking about how good kissing him felt made her weak in the knees. She was still a bit wobbly as she unlocked the door to her hotel room. Once inside, she flopped onto the bed and draped an arm over her eyes. Memories of the afternoon played in her mind and she had to admit to herself that she wanted to see him again.

There was a knock on her door. Sighing, Tiffany pushed herself off the comfortable mattress and opened the door. As expected, her sister was standing on the other side.

"Well?" Stephanie asked, walking around Tiffany and into the room. She took a seat on the chair and leaned her elbow on the desk. "How was your date?"

Tiffany shrugged and sat back on the bed. "It was okay. I guess. Nothing to write home about."

"Liar. I can see the sparkle in your eyes." Stephanie pulled her chair next to the bed and stared at Tiffany. "Start talking."

Unable to keep up her facade of indifference, Tiffany grinned. "I had a wonderful time. Ellis is a great guy."

"Tell me everything. Don't leave out a single detail."

"There's not all that much to tell. We walked around the park and ate lunch together. We need to check out the place where he got ribs by the way."

Stephanie waved her hand, clearly not deterred. "Okay. But you're holding back. I don't want to talk about food. How did being with Ellis make you feel?"

Tiffany sighed. She should have known that Stephanie would see through her. She'd always been smart that way. "I like him. I even kissed him, so you don't have to ask about that."

"It must have been good for you to just blurt it out like that."

Tiffany grew hot as she recalled the feel of Ellis's lips pressed against hers and she brushed her hand against her suddenly damp forehead. "It was. But don't get any ideas. It doesn't mean anything other than the fact that the man has had lots of practice. Although where he found women to experiment with in this tiny town is beyond me."

"If he's as great as you said, finding willing women wouldn't be hard."

"I didn't say he was great," Tiffany clarified. "And I know where you're going, so just pump your brakes before your imagination gets too far down the road."

"I'm not doing anything," Stephanie said innocently. But they were more than sisters. They were friends. Tiffany knew Stephanie too well to be fooled by a sweet smile.

"Yes, you are. You're dreaming of a wedding and happily-ever-after."

"And if I was? What's wrong with that?"

"Nothing. If that's what someone wants. Married life and motherhood look good on you. But it's not for me. I'm perfectly happy with my single life. I have a successful business that I took from a dream to a reality. I have good friends and a great family. My life is happy and fulfilling. I'm not missing out on a thing. I don't know why you don't believe me."

"Do you really want to know why?" Stephanie asked, a challenge in her voice.

Despite the dread that suddenly filled her stomach, Tiffany nodded. Stephanie never gave an unsolicited opinion, but if you opened the door, she would definitely walk through it. And she would tell you the unadulterated truth. "Say what you think. Why do you think I want a man in my life?"

"Because you were so happy when you were engaged to that jerk. You were looking forward to getting married and starting a family. Once you found out that he wasn't who he pretended to be, you were heartbroken. Anyone would be. And gun-shy. Again, that was expected. But it has been years. Just because you fell off the horse doesn't mean you don't ever get back on."

"You've been married to the rodeo star for too long. You know I've never been on a horse and don't intend to."

Stephanie shook her head. "You know what I mean. Don't let one liar break your heart so badly it never heals. Love is a wonderful thing. You knew it then, so you should know it now."

"I do. And I'm not saying that I won't fall in love again one day. But not now. And when I do, it won't be with Ellis Corey. His roots go as deep in this town as mine do in Bronco. There is no way he would ever leave and no way I could ever stay. Since that's the case, there's no reason for either of us to put our feelings out there just to have them get hurt. But that won't stop us from having fun while it lasts."

"That's all very logical. Unfortunately for you, the

heart is emotional. Look at me and Geoff. We're definitely opposite. He thrives in the spotlight and I would much rather live a quiet life where nobody knows who I am or cares to find out. But we fell in love. So we compromise."

"That works for you. But there's no need for me to compromise. I'm not in love with Ellis and don't plan on being. *We're just having fun.*"

Stephanie stood up. "Famous last words, dear sister."

Tiffany watched as her sister walked away. It was more than words. It was her plan and she intended to stick to it.

Chapter Three

Ellis opened the front door to his parents' house and stepped inside the familiar hallway. His and his siblings' high school graduation photos were hung on the walls and the entry table was filled with framed snapshots from his childhood. Laughter filled the air and he followed the sound through the house to the kitchen. Though the house had a perfectly good living room and an equally good family room complete with a big-screen television and plenty of comfortable seating, everyone tended to congregate in the kitchen, sitting around the table or the large granite island. Even before his parents renovated their kitchen, it had been a favorite gathering place for him and his siblings. From the time they were able to pour milk into a measuring cup or stir bowls of dry ingredients, they'd been expected to help their mother prepare meals. As a result they were all great cooks.

"Hey," his sister, Michelle, the only girl and baby of the family, said, coming over and giving him a hug. "How was your date?"

"Do I even want to know how you know about that?" Ellis asked.

Michelle gave him a saucy grin. “I have eyes and ears everywhere.”

“The nosy ones usually do,” Tristan added drily. He was two years younger than Ellis and the two of them—along with their eldest brother, Shane—had always been thick as thieves.

“Hey, no picking on the baby,” Aaron, the youngest brother, said. Predictably he defended Michelle. Aaron and Michelle were each other’s best friends. When their parents had brought Michelle home from the hospital twenty-seven years ago, two-year-old Aaron had taken one look at the tiny infant and designated himself as her guardian. Even now, he took that role of protector seriously.

“I wasn’t,” Tristan denied, raising his hands in surrender as he laughed.

“No, he was just helping Ellis avoid answering the question,” Michelle said as she poured milk into the potatoes she was mashing.

“You picked up on that,” Ellis said, then sighed. “It was actually good. Tiffany is sweet and surprisingly funny.”

“Who’s she?” Aaron asked. “I thought I knew every eligible woman in town. None of them are named Tiffany.”

“She’s a visitor,” Ellis said reluctantly, knowing there would be no easy way to end this conversation. He should have known better than to open the door by answering Michelle’s question. Now his entire family would be expecting details about his date and weighing in on his marital status. Fortunately, Tristan and

Aaron were still single and he could count on them to side with him. But if his mother and Michelle had their way, they would be walking him down the aisle by the end of summer. His father, Joseph, would keep his own counsel. He generally stayed out of his children's romantic affairs, saying he preferred to focus his attention on his marriage. Shane was a wild card. In the past, he could be counted on to form a united front with the brothers. Now that he was engaged, Ellis had no idea whose side he would come down on. But that's what made Sunday dinners at the Corey house so much fun. You never knew what would happen so you had to stay on your toes.

"Really?" Michelle asked. "Tell us more."

"After we get the food on the table," Patty, his mother, said, handing a platter containing a delicious smelling roast to Joseph to carry into the dining room. Without needing directions, Ellis and his siblings grabbed the bowls of side dishes and followed their parents.

Once they were seated and the food had been blessed, Ellis turned to Shane. "Where's Remi? I thought she would be here for dinner."

"She and her sisters are competing this weekend. She'll be back in the morning."

"Speaking of seeing someone in the future," Michelle said, "are you planning on seeing Tiffany again?"

Ellis didn't bother pointing out that neither he nor Shane said anything remotely like that. "Yes. I'm going to ask her to go out with me again. No, I won't be reporting back to you."

"So I won't get a chance to meet her and warn her away?" Her eyes danced with mischief.

"Nope. No warning is necessary. We're just having fun. Neither of us is looking for anything permanent. Remember, she's only here temporarily. When she leaves town that will be the end of things." He said the words, meant them even, but something inside him didn't particularly like the idea of ending things with Tiffany, especially when they had barely gotten started. But that's what he'd agreed to do. What he planned to do. "Now can we please talk about something else?"

His family exchanged glances and then, as one, turned to look at him. His mother spoke for all of them. "Of course."

After that they changed the subject, discussing everything from ranch business to the upcoming Dinosaurs Days. Though he tried to play it cool with his family, Ellis was excited about seeing Tiffany again. Perhaps he could convince her to participate in Dinosaur Days while she was in town. That way she might come to see Tenacity in a different light. He didn't know why it mattered to him that Tiffany viewed Tenacity favorably. It just did. Not because he wanted her to move here so they could continue their relationship. He wasn't planning on building a life with her. But he wouldn't be opposed to sharing a few more of those amazing kisses with her. Just remembering how good it felt to hold her in him arms was so distracting that he forgot to chew before he swallowed and he choked.

"Are you okay?" Shane asked, pounding Ellis on the back.

"Just swallowed wrong."

His brother gave him a hard stare, as if he knew Ellis was holding back. Maybe. But there was no way Shane could know *what* he'd been thinking. And Ellis wouldn't tell him. He wasn't sure his brother wouldn't make more of Ellis wanting to spend time with Tiffany than was there. Better safe than sorry.

After indulging in his mom's homemade raspberry cheesecake and a scoop of vanilla ice cream, Ellis and his siblings cleared the table and loaded the dishwasher so Patty could sit and relax. Though he was usually one of the last to leave, Ellis was feeling a bit restless, so he hugged his parents, told his siblings goodbye and headed for his home.

The ranch was large enough for each of the kids to have their own houses on their own sizable plot of land. Although Ellis enjoyed spending time with his family, he liked having a place of his own. He'd had to share a bedroom growing up, which meant compromising on everything from the color of the walls to the placement of the beds and dressers, so he liked being able to decorate his house to suit his own style. Every piece of art hanging on the wall had been chosen by him as had every stick of furniture and area rug. Now though, he didn't experience the satisfaction he usually felt when he stepped inside. The house echoed with emptiness as if something vital was missing. Or someone. That was ridiculous. This was his home. His sanctuary. Even so, he wished that Tiffany was here with him. His longing was so strong that he could practically see her sitting beside him on the couch as they listened to music or watched TV.

The silence in his house was suddenly deafening, so he grabbed his keys, got back into his truck and headed down the road to town. He needed something to distract him so he could get these unwanted thoughts of Tiffany out of his mind. When he reached Tenacity, he headed straight to the Grizzly Bar. Tiffany hadn't seemed impressed when he described the place to her, so he didn't have to worry about running into her tonight.

He grabbed a beer and then leaned against the bar and watched as two old guys played a game of pool. It was obvious that they were good friends. They talked a lot in between shots, with one starting the story and the other finishing it.

Deciding to stick around for a while, Ellis added his name to the chalkboard. There were three people ahead of him waiting to play the winner, but he wasn't in a hurry. There was nothing waiting for him at home other than the silence that he'd run away from. When it was his turn, Ellis grabbed his favorite stick, took his place at the table, nodded to his opponent and broke the balls. As a serious player, Ellis didn't talk during the game. Normally he was able to focus, but today he missed shots he could ordinarily make blindfolded.

It was no surprise when his opponent won. Ellis's mind was elsewhere. Specifically on Tiffany Brandt. If she could occupy his mind so fully after only one date and knock him completely off-kilter, perhaps it would be wise not to see her again.

But was he going to walk away from her? Absolutely

not. He was going to spend as much time with her as their schedules allowed. Clearly he wasn't his parents' smartest child.

"Are you sure you don't mind taking my place today?" Stephanie asked on Monday morning. She and Geoff had committed to helping publicize Dinosaur Days and had several meetings with various groups scheduled this morning. But Melanie had woken up with a slight fever and had been clinging to her mother all morning. Stephanie hadn't wanted to leave her little girl, even with Tiffany. As a nurse, Stephanie was much better equipped to care for her little one than Tiffany would ever be.

"Of course not. Nobody can make a sick child feel better than her mother."

"Hey, I heard that," Geoff said, coming into the room and shooting a mock glare in Tiffany's direction. "I can make my sweetie feel better, can't I?"

Geoff bent over and kissed Melanie's flushed cheek. She grinned around her thumb and then leaned her head back against Stephanie's chest.

"You're a close second," Tiffany said.

"I suppose I could do worse than coming in second behind my wife." Geoff gently kissed Stephanie, then leaned his forehead against hers. "I'll be back as soon as I can."

Stephanie shook her head. "Don't rush. She's just teething. I've already given her something for the pain. We'll be fine while you're gone."

Watching her sister and brother-in-law together made

Tiffany's heart ache with intense longing. She didn't begrudge Stephanie the happiness that she'd found with Geoff. Stephanie was a genuinely good person. Nobody deserved to be loved more than she did. But as much as Tiffany denied it, deep down she yearned for the kind of relationship that Stephanie and Geoff had. She would give anything to have a man look at her the way that Geoff looked at Stephanie. To have a man as devoted to his child as Geoff was to Melanie. But things hadn't worked out that way for her and she didn't imagine her fortunes would be changing in the future.

Though it was hard to admit, even to herself, her self-confidence was still shaken. Even now she didn't trust her judgment when it came to men. The man she'd thought she was going to marry had been two-timing her and she hadn't had a clue. She'd accepted his excuses for his long absences and hadn't given a second thought to the times she hadn't been able to reach him. She'd thought he'd been traveling for work when in reality, he'd been in the arms of another unsuspecting woman. Her blind faith had resulted in heartache. If there had been signs, she hadn't picked up on a single one of them. Looking back all these years later, she still couldn't figure out what she had missed.

Getting involved romantically with a man when she was unable to distinguish between a truly good man and a counterfeit—the real thing from a pretender—was too big a risk to take. She'd been burned badly and had barely managed to put herself back together again. No, until she was positive she could tell real gold from iron pyrite, she was leaving serious relationships alone.

"Thanks for stepping in today," Geoff said as they drove to the Tenacity Dinosaur Center and Park.

"No problem. I'm here to help in any way that I can."

"I appreciate that. But I also know that Tenacity isn't exactly your cup of tea."

"It's not that I don't like the people," Tiffany said quickly. "The few that I've met have been quite nice. It's just that the place is lacking some of the finer things that Bronco has to offer. Things that I can't imagine living without."

"You don't have to explain yourself to me. I'm married to your very glamorous sister. She also enjoys some of the finer things in life. All of which I'm more than happy to give her." He gave her a serious look. "But I hope you don't mind a little brotherly advice."

"Go ahead."

"Don't be so quick to sell this place short. It might not be much to look at, but appearances aren't everything. If you look past the shabby buildings, you might discover a few hidden gems."

Tiffany had a feeling he was talking about more than a saloon that sold delicious ribs. "If you say so."

When they reached their destination, Geoff parked between two older pickups and they went inside. Several people were already gathered, including the owner of Tenacity Feed and Seed and a couple of reporters from local TV stations and weekly newspapers. The mayor excused herself from the group before she walked over to Geoff and Tiffany. After welcoming them, she led them to the assembled guests who immediately stopped talking among themselves and gave Geoff their undivided attention.

"My daughter wasn't feeling well this morning, so my wife is staying with her. My sister-in-law Tiffany is here in Stephanie's place," Geoff said, explaining Tiffany's presence.

"I'm not sure how I can help, but I'll do my best," Tiffany said.

"Today we wanted to learn more about the softer side of Geoff Burris. The private side. His wife would have been our first choice, but as his sister-in-law, I'm sure you have a few stories you can share with us," a reporter who'd introduced himself as Roy said.

"Of course," Tiffany said.

Tiffany told stories about Geoff's kindness and how he volunteered his time to support the kids who lived in and around Bronco. She spoke about the free riding clinics he gave and his visits to local schools and hospitals. "Geoff is always available to help the youth. He has a real soft spot for them. He'll be doing the same at the Dinosaur Day festival where he'll also be conducting a riding clinic and doing several meet and greets."

"Thank you," Roy said. The other reporters nodded. "You've been very helpful and have given us more information about the side of Geoff Burris we don't often see."

"I'm glad I could help."

Once her part was over, the photographers began to take pictures of Geoff. Tiffany stood aside, absently noting how comfortable he was in front of the cameras, talking and joking with the photographers. When the shoot was over, Geoff went on to talk to the organizers about the rodeo. As rodeo's biggest star, he'd competed in numerous events and exhibitions over the years, so he knew the best way to draw a big crowd while simultaneously giving the audience the best bang for their buck.

Since this was out of her wheelhouse, Tiffany simply sat back and listened. Her mind unexpectedly strayed to Ellis and she smiled. She'd had such a good time with him. In her experience, men who were as handsome as he was were often self-centered. He hadn't been at all. He was self-deprecating and more interested in learning about her than talking about himself.

Tiffany thought about the kiss they'd shared and she immediately felt warm all over. She'd kissed many men in her life, but not one of them had ever made her feel the way that one had. She hadn't spent hours reliving the experience and longing for a repeat. An emotion that she was determined not to feel again tried to awaken but she squashed it. She was determined to ignore that feeling. Maybe that would make it go away.

Once the meetings were finished, Geoff and Tiffany said their goodbyes and walked back to the truck. Geoff unlocked the doors but Tiffany didn't get inside.

"Is something wrong?" Geoff asked.

"No. You go on back to the inn. I think I'll take your advice and look for hidden gems in town."

"That's not exactly what I meant," Geoff said.

"I know. But I feel like stretching my legs."

He stared at her for a moment, as if unsure whether to leave her alone. Geoff took his position as brother-in-law seriously.

"I'll be fine."

"Okay. Have a good time," he said. He opened his door. Before getting in the truck he looked at her. "Call me if you need me."

"I will." Tiffany waited until he had driven off before starting down the street. She'd gone a few blocks when she came upon Strom and Son Feed and Farm Supply. The building was well-kept and even had nice landscaping, but in Tiffany's mind it didn't qualify as a gem—hidden or otherwise. The door opened and Ellis stepped out. One look at him was all it took to make Tiffany's pulse race. Now he could be characterized as a gem.

"Ellis." His name burst from her lips before she had a chance to disguise her pleasure.

He smiled at her, his eyes dancing with delight. "Hi. I didn't expect to see you today."

"Surprise," she said.

"Yes, indeed. And it's a great one."

"I've been doing rodeo stuff with Geoff. I'm all finished now so I decided to take a walk and look around town."

"I thought you were here to watch the baby."

"That was the plan. But Melanie wasn't feeling good this morning, so Stephanie stayed with her and I went with Geoff."

"How are you going to spend the rest of the day?"

"I don't have any plans. What about you?"

"I just placed an order for some supplies. Do you want to have lunch with me?"

"Don't you have to get back to the ranch?"

He shrugged. "Even ranchers have to eat."

"I suppose that's true. Where do you want to go?"

"How about Castillo's? Their food is authentic and delicious. Or if you want, we can go out of town."

Before Tiffany could reply, a man walked up and shook Ellis's hand. "How's it going, Ellis?"

Ellis smiled. "No complaints, Harvey. How about you?"

"Same." Harvey nodded and smiled at Tiffany and then continued on his way.

"Let's go to Castillo's," Tiffany said when they were alone again. "I've gone there a couple of times and I absolutely love their food. The staff was great, too."

"Hop in my truck and we'll be there in half a minute."

Tiffany nodded and climbed inside. The interior was spotless, something she wouldn't have expected given that it was a work truck. She appreciated a man who took good care of his property.

As promised, they were seated in Castillo's in minutes. The storefront restaurant was small and cozy, if a little on the dark side. The dining room consisted of two rows of wooden booths separated by a narrow aisle. The aroma of grilling chicken, onions and peppers filled the air and Tiffany's mouth watered in anticipation. She picked up her menu, printed on simple white card stock. Everything about the place was unpretentious, but from what she'd already eaten, Tiffany believed the food was worthy of a Michelin star.

After perusing the menu, they placed their orders. In a moment, the server was back with their beverages.

Tiffany took a sip of her cold soda. “So, how are things on the ranch?”

“Good.”

“What kind of ranch does your family have?”

“Cattle.” Ellis leaned back in his chair. His eyes took on a faraway look. “My great-great-great grandfather, Cyrus Corey, founded the Circle C when he moved to Montana with the Homestead Act of 1862. He started with one hundred and sixty acres. He and my great-great-great grandmother had six sons and two daughters. After a while, Cyrus and two of his sons moved to Butte to mine copper, but the others stayed on the land. Initially they sold horses to the US army, then they switched to cattle.

“The ranch passed down from generation to generation, with each one buying acreage when they could. Ranching isn’t for everyone and several of my ancestors left to make their fortunes in other places. Eventually the land came to my grandfather, Otis. He worked his fingers to the bones in order to keep the ranch above water. When he and my grandmother got married, she worked right alongside him. Their kids eventually joined them. Their hard work paid off and the ranch grew more successful over the years. My parents bought out my uncles and grandparents.”

“Do your grandparents still live on the ranch?”

“No. They moved to a little house in Tenacity five years ago.”

“Is this the grandmother that is co-owner of the day-care?”

“Yes. Although she has several trustworthy employees, my grandmother is a hands-on person. She spends a lot of time there. It's a lot easier for her to get there from town. Of course, she and Grandpa still have their house on the ranch. They spend time there over the holidays or when my grandfather feels the need to go fishing."

"How many more acres did your family buy over time?" Though Tiffany didn't intend for this relationship with Ellis to last, she was curious about his life and genuinely interested in hearing about the ranch.

"One hundred and thirty acres. The ranch now is nearly twice the size as when Cyrus started it. Every one bought with the sweat of our family's brow."

"You sound proud."

"I am incredibly proud of my family and what they've achieved over the years. They not only survived, but thrived when so many other ranches went belly-up. Ranching isn't easy by any stretch of the imagination. When my grandfather took over from his father and uncle, there were very few people around and not much to do for entertainment. It was a very lonely life. Now it's less so with Tenacity being close by. There are places for ranchers to gather and shoot pool or play cards or just hang out. Places to listen to live music and dance."

"Really? In Tenacity?"

"Yes."

"I love live music," Tiffany said. "In fact, I go to a few concerts every year."

"In Bronco?"

"Sometimes. But for all of its amenities, it's still a small town. The big stars don't include it in their tours.

If there's someone I really want to see, I find a city that I want to visit where they're performing and go see them there. I make a short vacation of it. Since I love traveling, it's a win-win."

"I imagine it is."

Tiffany leaned her hand into her palm and glanced at Ellis. He was dressed in a plaid shirt and faded jeans that fit as if they'd been tailored specifically for him. As usual, there was a smile on his face that reflected an inner contentment. "Tell me about life on the ranch. What are your days like?"

"They start early," he said. There was a bowl of homemade chips on the table and Ellis took one, dipped it into the salsa and ate it before continuing. "My siblings and I live on the ranch. We each have our own houses, but my mother always makes a big breakfast for anyone who wants to stop by. We just need to let her know the day before so she'll know how much food to prepare. I eat breakfast there most mornings. Then we get to work. There are vaccinations to be given, cattle drives and branding. And of course feeding. We need to make plans to get the cattle to market. Every day is different so it never gets boring."

"Do you ride horses?"

"Sometimes. You know, if you want, you can spend the day with me." His voice sounded cautious as if he didn't want Tiffany to read too much into the offer. "That will give you a more accurate picture than anything I say. Plus you'll have a lot of fun."

"I wish I could," Tiffany said honestly. "But I have

Melanie to think about. I wouldn't feel comfortable bringing her with me."

"The invitation is an open one. You can visit whenever it's convenient for you."

Tiffany was nodding when a man and woman walked over to them. Ellis stood and smiled as he greeted them. "Ryder. Ella. It's good to see you. Let me introduce you to my new friend, Tiffany Brandt. Tiffany, this is Ryder Trent, a fellow rancher and his better half, Ella McIntyre, who is also our town librarian."

"Hello," Tiffany said, glancing at the couple. Although this was her first time seeing them, it was obvious from the way they smiled at each other and their gentle touches that they were in love. As a florist who regularly crafted bouquets for bridal parties and centerpieces for wedding receptions and anniversary parties, she'd developed a sixth sense about these things. She could tell whether a couple was going to last through the tough times or whether they would crumble before they reached their first anniversary. It was apparent that Ryder and Ella's love was real. Strong. They were definitely the kind who would be welcoming children and grandchildren together. Tiffany might not be able to find Mr. Right, but she was always pleased when she met couples who were truly in love. It was needed confirmation that real love actually did exist.

"It's nice to meet you," Ella said, sweeping a lock of her blond hair behind her ear. Her smile was warm and Tiffany felt as if she'd just made a friend. Tiffany noticed the way Ella's eyes darted between her and Ellis. Clearly Ella was putting two and two together and coming up with romance, the way the newly in love tended to do. “Are you new to town?”

“I’m visiting with my sister and her family.”

“Her brother-in-law is Geoff Burris,” Ellis said.

“Really? We can’t wait to see him compete at the rodeo,” Ryder said. “We already have our tickets.”

“It’s going to be a great time,” Tiffany said.

At that moment, the server arrived with their meals.

“We’ll let you eat. It was nice meeting you, Tiffany. Enjoy your visit,” Ella said as she and Ryder walked to their table.

“You’re quite popular in town,” Tiffany said when she and Ellis were alone. “Is there anyone you don’t know?”

He laughed. “There are quite a few, actually. Although I tried to meet them all. I recently ran for mayor. Since nobody is calling me Mr. Mayor, you can see how the election turned out.”

“Was this your first foray into politics?” Tiffany asked.

Ellis noted the lack of pity in her voice, something he was grateful for. He couldn’t take another well-meaning sympathetic smile or pat on the hand. He’d initially run for mayor on an impulse. Oh, he had given it some thought—it had been more than a lark—but a career in politics hadn’t been a lifelong goal of his. He’d always been civic-minded and had voted in every election since he’d turned eighteen. And he’d always donated to campaigns and volunteered to help his preferred candidates. But that had been the long and short of his involvement in politics. Until his failed mayoral run. There was work to be done to make this town thrive and he thought he was the best person to do it. Apparently the people of Tenacity thought otherwise. "Yes. First and last."

"What made you decide to toss your cowboy hat into the ring?"

He shrugged. "Why does anyone run for office?"

He'd thrown that answer out there in a flippant attempt to avoid revealing his disappointment and hurt feelings, so he was surprised when Tiffany answered thoughtfully.

"I suppose there are as many reasons as there are people. But on the whole I think there are two broad categories. One group wants to help their fellow citizens and make their lives better. The other wants to help themselves, using the power and influence that comes with the office for personal gain."

"I'm definitely in the first group."

Tiffany smiled. "I had already figured that out."

Ellis sighed. "I wanted to help the people of Tenacity. I still do. There are a lot of good people living here. People who work hard every day and deserve to benefit from that labor. This is a great place to live and more people need to know about it. But we need to attract more industry. People need good jobs. I believe with the right leadership—creative leadership that thinks outside the box—we can attract those businesses and provide those jobs and make people see a future here."

He heard the fervor in his voice and forced himself to take a deep breath. "Sorry. I got carried away."

“Don’t be. That is some stump speech. I’m surprised that you didn’t win the election.”

So was he. And he’d been heartbroken as well. “It was a disappointment. But life goes on. The people made a choice and I have to live with it.” He’d said the same thing many times in the months since the election, but it had taken quite a while before he no longer felt the sting of rejection. That reaction had been out of character for him. He generally was able to shrug off a loss and keep it moving. He knew he had a lot of things going for him—too many things for him to wallow in hurt feelings. That just showed how deeply disappointed he’d been. But bruised feelings wouldn’t stop him from helping the town he loved.

“That’s true. And it’s Tenacity’s loss. You would have made a great public servant.”

“Being mayor isn’t the only way I can serve the town and its people. I always try to help out whenever and wherever I can.”

“That attitude is impressive. It shows your real heart for the people. And your true purpose for running.”

“I really want the best for Tenacity.”

“I met Mayor Garrett, by the way. She seems to care about the town, too.”

“JenniLynn is a good person. She’s doing a good job as mayor. Despite the dirty trick that her husband played on her.”

Curiosity sparked in her dark eyes and she leaned closer, her voice lowered. Sexier. “What does that mean?”

Ellis leaned in closer, not because he was saying anything that he didn't want anyone to overhear—the entire town knew the sordid tale—but because he wanted to be nearer to Tiffany. "He actually colluded with another candidate to steal the election, if you can believe it. He didn't want JenniLynn to win."

"Wow. Her own husband did that. That takes betrayal to a whole new level. I don't know if I could stay married to someone who sabotaged me like that. How could I ever trust him again?"

"I misspoke. I should have said her *ex*-husband. They're divorced now."

Tiffany shook her head slowly, and her soft curls brushed her slender shoulders. "It's that kind of behavior that makes you think twice about falling in love and making yourself vulnerable. Is it really worth the risk?"

"Some people think so. Look at Ryder and Ella. They're happy."

"I was just thinking that they look like a couple who could make love last." Tiffany lifted her cup in toast. "Here's to Ella and Ryder."

As he joined the toast, a part of him wondered if there was lasting love in his future. Perhaps with Tiffany? He shut down that thought instantly. He wasn't looking for love, lasting or otherwise. Clearly, neither was she.

He was happy with his life just as it was. Wasn't he?

Chapter Four

"What are you doing for the rest of the day?" Ellis asked after they'd finished their enchiladas. Though he had work waiting for him back at the ranch, work that he usually enjoyed doing, he wasn't ready for the afternoon to end. Tiffany was really easy to talk to. He hadn't planned to go into details about the election and how disappointed he'd felt at losing. How at loose ends he occasionally still felt even after all this time. But once the words started pouring out of his mouth, he wasn't able to hold back. It was as if a dam had been broken, allowing everything to gush forth. Then, after seeing her reaction, he didn't want to stop. He'd wanted to tell her everything.

"I thought I would walk around town. See what else there is to see."

"Would you like company?"

"Sure. If you have the time. I feel like I'm taking you away from something important."

"Nothing that can't be done a couple of hours later." Or by his brothers. They covered for each other when necessary.

She smiled and he felt something tug at his heart.

That was ridiculous. They'd already talked about this. Neither of them was looking for a romantic relationship. That's why they were so right for each other. And if one day that should change for him, Tiffany was not the woman he would choose to be with. Not that there was anything wrong with her. With her clear brown skin, bright eyes and sexy smile, she was easily the most beautiful woman he'd ever laid eyes on. She was slender and slightly shorter than the women he usually dated, but that didn't detract from her appeal. And she had a sparkling personality with a quick wit. She was kind and sympathetic. In a word, she was perfect. *For someone else.* When he decided to settle down—and he had no doubt that he would at some point in the distant future—it would be with someone who was as rooted in Tenacity as he was. Someone who actually liked the town and intended to make it their home. Though Tiffany hadn't said anything too negative about Tenacity, he knew that she didn't feel the same way he did, nor was she about to leave Bronco.

As they walked down the street, Ellis tried to see the town through Tiffany's eyes. He could see that several of the buildings were showing their age. A facelift wouldn't hurt, he realized. But everything was clean. The pride the owners had in their businesses shone through. Would Tiffany see that?

When they reached the Little Cowpokes Daycare Center, Tiffany stopped. "This is the business that your grandmother co-owns, right?"

He nodded. The red brick building was one of the best maintained in town. There were welcoming flowers that changed with the seasons in concrete urns beside the front door.

"Would it be all right if we stopped in for a minute?"

"Sure. My grandmother loves when one of her grandkids drops in for a visit. But I have to warn you, she usually puts us to work. Don't be surprised if she hands you a cloth and has you sanitizing the table and chairs."

Tiffany smiled. "That sounds like something my grandmothers would do. They're not big on standing on formality."

More satisfied with her answer than he should have been, Ellis opened the door and stepped into a small hall. The inside door was locked and Ellis rang a bell. Lola, one of the employees, buzzed them in and Ellis and Tiffany stepped into the big room that opened onto several smaller ones. The kids were separated by age in the smaller rooms and ate and had group activities in this room.

"Hi," he said to Lola, who had been sweeping the floor. Now she leaned on a broom, looking from him to Tiffany as he introduced her. "Is my grandmother free?"

"Yes. She's in her office," Lola said as she resumed sweeping.

"Thanks." Ellis led Tiffany down a short, well-lit hall. The walls were decorated with the latest art projects that the students had created.

When they reached his grandmother's office, he knocked on her open door. Angela was sitting at her desk, working at her computer. Her framed college degree in early childhood education and awards that she'd received over the years hung from the walls. His grandmother had gone back to school when her children were grown and she regularly reminded everyone that it was never too late to achieve your goals.

She looked up and immediately smiled when she saw them. "Well, isn't this a nice surprise."

Angela walked around the desk and gave Ellis a long embrace.

"You always say that," he said, hugging her back.

"I always mean it." Angela looked at Tiffany. Ellis could read the questions in his grandmother's eyes and wondered if he'd made a mistake by bringing Tiffany here. He never brought a woman around his grandmother because he knew that she would start hearing wedding bells. So why had be brought Tiffany here today? Well, she'd asked and he couldn't exactly deny her request, could he?

Tiffany held out her hand. "Hi. I'm Tiffany Brandt. I'm visiting from Bronco and Ellis has been kind enough to show me around town. When he mentioned your daycare, I asked if we could visit."

"I see. Well, come sit down for a minute so we can get better acquainted. Then I'll show you around so you can see everything."

Ellis was trying to think of an excuse as to why they couldn't stay when Tiffany followed his grandmother over to the small sitting area. Angela took a chair and Tiffany sat on the love seat across from her. Having no choice, Ellis sat beside her. He took a bracing breath to prepare himself for his grandmother's interrogation and inhaled a lungful of Tiffany's sweet scent. She always smelled so good.

Like flowers and sunshine. And joy.

"Do you work with children?" Angela asked.

"No. I'm a florist. I actually own my own shop back home in Bronco."

"Really. How do you like it?"

"I love it." Tiffany's voice rang with pride and her eyes lit up. "It was a struggle in the beginning but it was worth it. There is nothing like knowing that I built my own business with nothing more than grit and hard work. Oh, and I like being my own boss."

Angela nodded in approval. She had always preached that it was important for a woman to have her own income, so he knew Tiffany just went up in Angela's estimation. Not that he was worried about Tiffany satisfying Angela's criteria. She wasn't auditioning for a place in his family. Even so, he liked watching as Tiffany and his grandmother chatted briefly about the pros and cons of being an entrepreneur.

"So what brings you to town?" Angela asked.

Tiffany quickly explained about helping out with her niece while her sister and brother-in-law helped plan and advertise the rodeo at Dinosaur Days.

"You're welcome to bring the little one here while you're in town. That is, if it's okay with her parents. And while you visit, you could teach the children about flowers and plants. We have a space out back that I'm planning to turn into a garden soon so I can teach the children how to grow flowers and vegetables. I've got a million ideas, but only two hands." Angela raised her hands as if to emphasize her point.

"I'd love to visit and help you with the children. But I

don't know how much help I'd be with Melanie around. She tends to be shy around new people. I would probably end up carrying her around all day."

"I see." Angela nodded slowly. Then she tapped her chin, a clear sign that she was thinking. "We're going to be participating in Dinosaur Days. Maybe you can help me then. If you have time. I have a project planned for the kids but I would welcome another."

"I'd love to. My sister won't need my help on that day so I'll be free. And I know just the thing. I can let the kids decorate flowerpots and then plant a bloom in it. It will be a nice introduction to your garden. I'll donate all the supplies of course."

"That sounds wonderful. I know my kids will love it." Angela paused, deep in thought. "I think some of the older kids in town might like it, too."

"Don't worry. I'll bring lots of flowers, pots and paint. Any kid who wants to participate will be welcome to do so. No one will be turned away."

"That sounds like a plan."

Angela picked up a brochure from her desk and handed it to Tiffany. "The daycare's telephone number and email are on here. I'll give you my cell number and personal email, too. Then give me yours. That way we can stay in touch and firm up the details."

Tiffany quickly scribbled her information on a pad and gave it to Angela who did the same.

Ellis stood. "I know that you're busy so we'll get out of your hair."

"I'll get all the items together and then contact you to make sure it works with your plans for the daycare,"

Tiffany said. "And I meant it when I said I'd help you with your garden. I love digging in the dirt. Just tell me when and I'll be here."

Angela smiled and gave Tiffany a hug. "You are a godsend. I knew I liked you the second I saw you."

Tiffany smiled. "The feeling is mutual."

"Do you have time to look at the yard?" Angela asked.

"Of course."

Angela gave them a quick tour of the daycare before leading them to the backyard. She pointed out the place in the lawn where she wanted the raised beds to be built. There was a lot of work to be done in order to make her vision a reality, but Ellis had no doubt that she would accomplish it.

"I'll look forward to hearing from you soon," Angela said as she led them to the front entry.

"You will," Tiffany said.

When Ellis and Tiffany were alone, he turned to her. "I hope you understand what you just did."

"Sure. I agreed to help your grandmother with Dinosaur Days and to help her with the daycare garden. I think they'll be a lot of fun. I'm looking forward to doing both."

He shook his head. "You are so adorably naive."

"Meaning?" She titled her head, looking sexier than she should have.

"My grandmother has matchmaking on her mind. I never bring women around her or any of the women in my family for this exact reason. She liked you. A lot.

If not, she wouldn't have invited you to help with her kids. She's very protective of them."

"I liked her. And I think that you're worrying about nothing."

"I didn't say I was worrying."

"You didn't have to. It's obvious that you're afraid that I'll get the wrong idea and start envisioning becoming a part of your family. Well, stop. That's the absolute last thing on my mind."

Tiffany hadn't intended to say anything about joining Ellis's family, but the words were out there now and there was no taking them back. Normally she was in control of herself, so this sudden lapse was disturbing. One time could be overlooked, but this made twice in only a few days. That meant trouble. It was a sign that her feelings for Ellis were growing, despite the fact that the two of them were completely mismatched. It wasn't as if she didn't like him. She did. It would actually be better for her if she liked him a little less. She would be leaving town for good after the rodeo. It wouldn't make sense to become attached when she was going to have to say goodbye soon. But it was hard to keep the walls around her heart strong when the more she was around him, the more things she discovered to admire about him.

But… Could he really be the hidden gem that Geoff mentioned? Or even the rarest thing of all—an honest man? Not that it mattered. She was still staying in the relationship-free zone where it was safe.

"No, I'm not worried about that. I'm used to my family," Ellis said.

"That's a relief." Tiffany looked him squarely in the eyes. "So what's the problem?"

"I don't want them to scare you off."

"You mean like run me out of town?" She couldn't keep the laughter from her voice. "I'm going home after the rodeo, remember?" Surprisingly, the thought of leaving Tenacity didn't excite her the way it had before she'd met Ellis. Now she wasn't as eager to get back to her newly renovated shop as she had been only days earlier. Why was that?

"No. I just mean she's likely to scare you into avoiding me. I don't want you to think that introducing you to my grandmother meant anything special. You know, like you were meeting the family matriarch."

"The thought never crossed my mind." But she knew where he was coming from. That's why she hadn't wanted him to meet Stephanie and Geoff. She didn't want him to get the wrong idea either.

"Good enough." Ellis stared at her for a long moment, as if trying to see inside her. Then his smile returned. It was never missing for long. "On that note, I suppose I should get back to the ranch. I'll drop you back at the inn."

As they drove, Tiffany's heart raced as she recalled the last time they'd parted. The way they'd kissed had never been far from her memory. It had been the kiss of a lifetime. Would he kiss her again? Even more, did she want him to?

That was easy to answer. Yes.

"I'll get your door," Ellis said, putting the truck into park.

"No need. I've got it." Tiffany turned to him, but when he made no move toward her, she opened her door and got out of his truck. It was only when she was sulking in her room that she realized she had no one to blame for the lack of a kiss but herself. She hadn't given him the kiss sign.

Perhaps that was for the best. She was really starting to like him. It was time to pump the brakes before it was too late.

The next few days passed quickly and Tiffany spent many enjoyable hours babysitting and playing with her niece. She and Ellis spoke briefly twice, but there'd been no time to get together. Now, it was the first day of Dinosaur Days, and she was filled with excitement. She was going to see Ellis today.

Tiffany and Angela had discussed their planned projects and had decided that it would be best if they had adjoining booths. That way the kids could spread out as they painted flowerpots with Tiffany and made puzzles with Angela. Tiffany figured that Ellis would be helping his grandmother at her booth. That's what family did. Even so, she expected that he would find time to stop over and see her. They might not have time to be alone, but at least they'd have a few minutes together.

The day was bright and sunny with a few billowy white clouds floating in the blue sky. It was the perfect day for an outdoor event. Hopefully that would lead to the big turnout that the organizers were hoping for.

Tiffany was wearing a pair of faded jeans and a blue

denim top with white stitches on the pockets that she knotted at her waist. It wasn't exactly high fashion, but since she would be around kids, paint and dirt, common sense overrode her desire to look stylish.

She brushed her hair over her shoulders and put on a white denim headband to keep it out of her face while she worked, then joined Stephanie and Geoff in their room. Geoff would be doing promotion for the rodeo and meeting with fans in a move designed to attract even more visitors. Stephanie planned to wander around with Melanie, taking in the sights.

"Only you could make denim look that good," Stephanie said. "You know, I have an extra cowboy hat if you want to wear it."

"Why would I want to do that?"

"To complete your outfit. You know, the whole cowgirl look. I even have an extra pair of cowboy boots if you want to go all out."

"You really have changed," Tiffany said, shaking her head. Stephanie had always been a fashionista. She'd had stylish boots of all colors, but not one pair of them had been cowboy boots. And the sister Tiffany had grown up with wouldn't have been caught dead in a cowboy hat. But that was before Stephanie had married the biggest star in rodeo. Now she was wearing a dove-gray cowboy hat and matching boots. "I never thought I would see the day."

"Neither did I. Yet here we are. Even Melanie is getting into the act." Stephanie pointed at the pink cowboy hat on the child's head, which was secured under her chin, and the matching boots on her tiny feet. "Of course, I'm not sure how long the boots will last. My child prefers to go barefoot."

Tiffany was about to decline the offer but she reconsidered. Ellis might like women who dressed in Western wear. Not that what he liked should matter to her. She didn't dress to please men. Still, she figured, she may as well go all in. "Sure. I'll take the boots and hat."

Stephanie's eyes widened in obvious surprise. Then, without saying a word, she opened the closet door and grabbed a pair of tan cowboy boots and a tan Stetson and held them out to Tiffany. After swapping her shoes for boots and her headband for the cowboy hat, Tiffany glanced at her reflection in the mirror. Not bad. It wasn't a look she would sport with any regularity, but when in Rome…

"You look even cuter, if that's possible," Stephanie said.

"You aren't fooling me for a second. You just don't want to be the only Brandt sister who's gone country," Tiffany said with a laugh.

"Guilty. But you do look nice." Stephanie whipped out her phone and, before Tiffany could protest, snapped a picture of her. Then she stepped beside Tiffany and took a selfie. "Just in case this never happens again, I want to document the occasion."

"More than likely you'll use this as blackmail material," Tiffany muttered.

"Thanks for the idea," Stephanie said. Her fingers flew over her phone. "I texted you copies."

Tiffany nodded. She would delete the pictures as soon as she could.

Geoff joined them and the three of them loaded her supplies in Geoff's truck and headed to the Dinosaur Center. When they arrived, Geoff helped Tiffany carry everything to her booth. Tiffany was surprised by the number of booths filling the area. The festival was much bigger than she had anticipated. There were a dozen food trucks beside tables and a kids' area with bouncy houses and face painters. Tenacity had gone all out.

She looked around her booth. There were two small square tables with four chairs set beneath them on the near side. A large rectangular table was on the far end. She and Geoff placed the boxes holding her supplies there.

"Do you need help setting up?" Geoff asked.

"No. I've got it. Besides, you need to get to your meet and greet."

"In that case, I'll leave you to it. Have fun." He tipped his hat and then walked away.

Tiffany looked at the pile of red and blue smocks, the buckets holding flowers, the gallons of paint and the terra cotta flowerpots and sighed. There was a lot of work to get done before the kids started streaming in.

"Do you need any help?"

Ellis's deep voice sent shivers down Tiffany's spine and she inhaled a calming breath before turning to face him. Even so, she was struck by how handsome he was. With rich brown skin, intelligent and kind eyes and dimples to die for, he was practically irresistible. His casual jeans and short-sleeved shirt did little to disguise his well-sculpted body. “As a matter of fact, I could use a pair of strong arms.”

Ellis flexed and his muscles bulged beneath his knit shirt. “Are these strong enough?”

Tiffany swallowed in an effort to keep from drooling. She would prefer to have those arms wrapped around her, holding her against his broad chest in a tight embrace, but since that wasn’t on offer, she nodded and gave him a cheeky grin. “I suppose those will do in a pinch.”

Ellis laughed. “You don’t fool me for a minute.”

“Really?”

“Yes, really.” He grabbed her by the waist and lifted her into the air, shocking a gasp from her. Then she began to laugh. Ellis spun her around in fast circles and Tiffany placed her hands on his strong shoulders to steady herself, noting just how firm they were. She inhaled and was treated to the scent of his subtle, slightly woodsy cologne. She had the urge to bury her face into his neck and breathe him in, but she resisted the temptation, unsure if she would be able to stop herself from giving into other temptations that were sure to follow. This was a family occasion and plenty of little ones would be coming to her booth. Their parents wouldn’t appreciate stumbling upon Ellis and Tiffany making out.

The sound of a microphone screeching in the distance filled the air followed by the mayor’s voice welcoming everyone to Dinosaurs Days, which put a temporary end to their game. Ellis spun in one last circle, then set Tiffany back on her feet. Slightly dizzy, she staggered and then leaned against his chest until the world gradually stopped spinning.

"I suppose we need to get things organized," Tiffany said, reluctantly easing out of Ellis's comfortable embrace. "The kids will be here before we know it."

"If you insist."

They set the small flowerpots on the tables, one in front of each chair. Then they set paintbrushes and plastic cups that would hold the paint in the middle of the table. She left the towels and cleaning supplies on the large table, beside the remaining pots and gallons of paint.

Tiffany looked around. "Now all I need is kids."

"Your wish has been granted," Ellis said. "Here come some now."

A woman with three children in tow stepped up to the booth. "Are you open?"

"Yes, I am." Tiffany smiled and put on a pink apron with the Tiffany in Bloom logo embroidered on the front and then squatted in front of the children. "I'm Tiffany and we're going to have a great time. What are your names?"

The biggest girl, who looked about six, introduced herself as Wendy and then introduced her younger sisters, Mindy and Mandy. "They're twins."

"I can see that." Tiffany helped the little girls put smocks over their clothes and led them to a table. Once the children were seated, Tiffany she showed them four completed pots to get their imaginations going. Then she gave each child a paintbrush and filled cups with paint. "You can paint your flowerpots any color or pattern you like. There is no right or wrong way. Then while the paint is drying, you can choose a flower to plant in them. Does that sound like fun?"

Mindy and Mandy looked at Wendy, who answered for all three of them. "Yes."

Tiffany stepped back and watched as the children worked, giving guidance when necessary, but otherwise she let the kids create their own masterpieces without comment. When the girls were finished painting, they placed their pots on the long table to dry. Then Tiffany led them to the flowers. As expected, Wendy and her sisters deliberated quite a while as they searched for the perfect blooms. By the time they'd each chosen the flower they wanted, the pots were dry. The kids held their flowers in the middle of the pots while Tiffany spooned in dirt and tamped it down.

"Ta-da!" Tiffany said, taking time to look into each girl's eyes. "Look at what you've done. You've started a little flower garden."

"We did?" Wendy whispered. Her voice was filled with awe.

"I like mine," Mandy said.

"Me, too," Mindy said

Tiffany smiled. Those were the only words the two youngest had spoken the entire time. Those quiet comments were as valuable as gold.

"I like them all. Now it's time to wash our hands." Tiffany poured warm, soapy water into shallow tubs and the kids laughed as they swished their hands around, getting most of the paint and dirt off. As expected, they splashed water all over the smocks and the table.

When their hands were dry, they picked up their flowerpots and headed to their waiting mother who oohed and aahed over them.

Then Tiffany waved goodbye and waited for the next kids to arrive.

Ellis watched as Tiffany interacted with the continuous line of children. He'd seen her with her niece, so he knew that she was kind. But being sweet to a family member—especially one so young—was expected. Having patience with strangers who smeared paint all over your jeans, as a little boy was currently doing in his attempt to get Tiffany's attention, took a special kind of person.

Stooping down, Tiffany smiled into the child's face, giving him her full attention, something Ellis had watched her do countless times over the past couple of hours.

"I need more green paint," the boy said, pointing to a tiny spot on his flowerpot that wasn't covered with paint.

"I see, Timmy," Tiffany said, leading him back to the table. If she was bothered by the kid-sized handprint on her jeans, she didn't show it. She simply poured more green paint into the empty cup and set it on the table in front of the boy. "Here you go."

"Thank you," Timmy said, dipping his brush into the paint and getting back to work.

A little girl wanted Tiffany to help her pour dirt into her pot while another wanted Tiffany to help her to pick out the "prettiest flower in the world" for her mommy.

Though Ellis could watch Tiffany work with the kids all day and never get tired, he was here to help. He emptied the basin of dirty water, sanitized it, then filled it with clean, soapy water before wiping paint off the chairs. Even as he cleaned, he found his eyes following Tiffany. There was something about her that was impossible for him to ignore. Especially in these tight quarters.

Dressed in jeans that cupped her round bottom and a shirt that showed off her slender torso and perky breasts—despite the apron she wore—she took his breath away. She'd long since removed her hat. Though he liked the way it had framed her pretty face, he loved the way her dark hair cascaded over her shoulders, shifting from side to side whenever she turned her head.

"That's beautiful," Tiffany said to a little boy who'd just planted his flower in his pot and was holding it up to her. Her voice was warm and the little boy grinned at her. It was too bad that she didn't want a commitment because she would make a great mother. To *someone else's* children. Not his. He wasn't looking to create a family with Tiffany. Their relationship, though satisfying, was temporary.

"She's really good with the kids, isn't she?" his grandmother said, coming to stand beside him. She'd come into the booth several minutes ago to make sure everything was going well. Angela and one of the other teachers had been helping kids put together dinosaur puzzles and color dinosaur pictures in the booth next to theirs. He'd intended to stop by and help but he hadn't been able to tear himself away from Tiffany's side.

Ellis turned, grateful for the distraction. He didn't

want to start thinking about Tiffany and children. But that didn't mean he couldn't acknowledge her good qualities. "Yes, she is. She's a natural."

Angela gave him a long, searching look as if trying to discover what his words were hiding from her. He kept his expression neutral, doing his best to disguise his confused emotions. Angela nodded. "But then, the moment I met her, I knew she would be. I'm glad to see that you picked up on that, too."

"Don't get any ideas," he warned. He knew how Angela thought and how single-minded she could be. "We're friends. *Just* friends."

"The relationships that can stand the test of time start out as friendships. Do you think your grandfather and I just took one look at each other and fell in love?"

Ellis shrugged. "I really hadn't given it much thought."

"Of course you didn't. Most people your age don't think about their grandparents as real people. You probably don't even know our names. To you we're Grandma and Grandpa. The people who you ran to for protection when you got in trouble with your parents. And in your case that was quite a lot. So let me set the record straight. Otis and I were friends long before we started dating. In fact, I even went on a couple of dates with one of his friends. Obviously nothing came of that. A few months later, I started to see your grandfather as a potential mate. It took him longer to see me as more than a friend. But then I was always patient." She grinned. "And persuasive."

"I didn't know any of this."

"Well, now you do."

"I'm assuming there's a reason you told me this. Other than letting me know that you had a boyfriend before Grandpa, that is. Or should I call him Otis?"

Angela grabbed his cheeks. "You always were a smart aleck. Why don't you try calling him that to his face and see what happens?"

He laughed. When his grandmother released his face, he leaned over and kissed her on the cheek. "I think I'll pass."

"That's probably for the best," Angela said. "I need to get back to my booth. Dinosaur puzzles wait for no man."

"Hold on. Aren't you going to tell me what I'm supposed to learn from your story?" Ellis asked.

Angela grinned, then glanced at Tiffany. "No. But you're a smart kid. You'll figure it out."

Shaking his head, Ellis turned his attention back to Tiffany. She might be great with kids, but that didn't change anything between them. They were only friends and no amount of patience or persuasion would change that fact.

Chapter Five

"That went well," Tiffany said. She'd spent the past five hours working in her booth having the time of her life and was now feeling quite satisfied with herself. Though the craft had been intended for the little ones and she'd expected elementary grade kids to stop by, she'd been pleasantly surprised when quite a few middle schoolers asked if they could also make a project. Even a dozen or so young teenagers had come, grinning boys making gifts for girls that they liked, and girls painting pots for themselves.

"You sound surprised," Ellis said, coming to stand beside her. He'd spent most of the day helping her, but she still wasn't immune to the effect that he had on her. Her senses had been on high alert from the moment he'd offered his strong arms to her that morning.

"I suppose I am. You never know with these type of events. You can have a huge turnout or spend hours twiddling your thumbs, hoping someone would stop by. I'm just glad that I had enough supplies." She held up one empty flowerpot. "This is all that remains."

"Let me have it," Ellis said, holding out his hand.

"What are you going to do with it?"

"Wear it as a hat."

"What?"

He grinned. "I'm going to do the same thing everyone else did. Unless you had plans other plans for it."

"No. It's all yours."

She silently handed him the pot, then leaned against the table so she could watch him work. He studied the paintbrushes, finally choosing one with the least amount of paint smeared on the handle. He rinsed it and glanced at her. "What's your favorite color?"

"I don't have one."

"Of course you do. Everyone does."

She grinned and placed a hand on her hip. "I'm not like everyone else. Or hadn't you noticed?"

"Oh, I've noticed. You are definitely one of a kind."

"And this one of a kind woman doesn't have a favorite color."

"Then do you have a *least* favorite color? Or one you don't like?"

"Nope. I like them all."

He sighed. "I don't think that's possible."

She thrust out her hands. "Of course it is. I like all colors. They each have their own unique beauty. Kind of like people."

"I suppose you don't have a favorite flower either."

"I don't have *one* favorite flower, but I do have several that I adore."

He dried the brush on a towel and then picked up two cups with paint in them. Then he looked at her as if expecting something more from her. "Are you going to tell me what they are or is it a state secret?"

"I'm a florist, not a political operative. I don't have state secrets."

"Then there should be no reason for you not to answer my question."

"Right. I love tulips. Yellow ones are my favorite. Tulips are so delicate, but beautiful. They don't last long, but that just makes them even more special. They're like a spring fling. You enjoy them, but they're gone before you can get tired of them." She glanced at Ellis. He was painting, but it was clear that he was listening to her. "And hyacinths. I love the way they smell. Purple are my favorites. And of course roses. You can never go wrong with pink roses."

"And you don't have any of those flowers here."

"Nope. I have daisies, carnations and daffodils. But I like them a lot, too."

"Of course you do." His voice was dry and she smiled. He turned back to his project, dabbing the brush into the paint, then smoothing it onto the flowerpot. He worked quickly yet carefully and she watched mesmerized as his muscles moved ever so slightly beneath his shirt. When she realized that she was gawking like a lovestruck teenager, she turned away and got back to cleaning the booth.

Ellis sang softly as he worked, and Tiffany found herself entranced by the sound of his melodic voice. It was deep and rich and turned her stomach into a gooey mess. Try as she might, no amount of sternly worded reasons why she needed to keep her distance from him did anything to stem the attraction that was blossoming inside her.

The space was tight and every time they'd bumped into each other during the day, she'd felt a shock that had sent tingles skipping down her spine. She had begun to enjoy the feeling just a little too much. Though she'd told herself to stay on the opposite side of the booth whenever possible, he was like a magnet drawing her to him and she was powerless to resist.

"I'm done. I didn't pile on the paint as thick as the kids did, so it should be ready for a flower by the time we load up this stuff."

She frowned. "That may be a bit of a problem. Geoff dropped me off and I don't have a clue where he parked. Even if I did, I don't have keys to his truck. I suppose I could call him."

"There's no reason to interrupt his day. We can put everything in my truck."

"You don't mind?"

"I wouldn't have offered if I did. Let me grab a flower or two and pour some dirt into the flowerpot first."

Tiffany stepped aside, watching as Ellis deliberated as much as the kids had over flowers, his brow drawn in concentration. There weren't many left to choose from and some of them were worse for wear. After a minute, he picked up two daisies and set to work potting them.

Tiffany closed the bag of soil and set it in a box beside the half-empty paint containers. She gathered up the remaining flowers, scribbled *free to a good home* and drew a smiley face on a sheet of paper, then set everything outside her booth. When she looked up, Ellis was standing there, his creation in his hands. He offered it to her.

"For me?" she asked, irrationally touched. She'd figured that he was making the craft for his mother or grandmother.

"Who else?"

Her stomach flip-flopped and she couldn't wipe the goofy grin from her face. "Thank you."

"Hasn't anyone ever given you flowers?" he asked. His tone was filled with shock as if her reaction had surprised him.

She shrugged, trying to cover her initial reaction. "I'm a florist. I suppose people believe that since I work with flowers I wouldn't want to receive them as a gift. To them it's like taking a chef out to dinner." In truth, she would have loved receiving the occasional bouquet. Heck, she would be happy with a bunch of wild flowers pulled from the side of the road if the right person offered them to her.

"Well, then I'm happy to be the first."

"I'll treasure them always." She tried to inject a bit of levity into her voice, but she wasn't quite able to mask the sincerity that revealed the depths of her feeling. It was ridiculous to be so affected since she'd bought everything but she still felt warm all over.

He nodded, clearly pleased with himself. He gestured to his creation. "You hold on to that and I'll put this stuff in my truck."

Carrying her flower like a diamond, and grinning from ear to ear, Tiffany followed Ellis to his pickup. Once everything was stowed in the truck bed, he turned to her. "If you're not in a hurry, how about we get in on some of the fun? The Dinosaur Days festival has a lot to offer."

"That's a great idea. Where should we go first?"

"I don't know about you, but I could do with some food."

Tiffany nodded. "I could eat."

A section of the park had been turned into a food court. Food trucks selling everything from walking tacos to fried rice to barbecued turkey wings were placed near long tables. Crowds of people were sitting at those tables, talking and eating, as little kids raced around. Ellis and Tiffany considered the offerings, then chose corn dogs and soft drinks so they could walk as they ate. They stopped at several vendor booths. The wares were quite impressive, especially for a small-town event, and though Tiffany didn't intend to buy anything, she ended up purchasing a pair of one-of-a-kind earrings and a handmade shawl. She had no idea where she would wear the shawl, but it was too beautiful to leave behind.

As they meandered, Tiffany noticed that everyone they passed either nodded a greeting to Ellis or stopped to talk with him.

"I know I said it before, but you are definitely popular," Tiffany said. "Everyone seems to like you."

"You should definitely follow their lead. After all, everyone can't be wrong."

"I was raised to blaze my own path."

"There's nothing stopping you from blazing a path in my direction."

Tiffany smiled. That did sound good. Without taking time to think, she slipped her arm through his. He gave her arm a gentle squeeze, then they continued strolling together.

A large sign had been posted in the middle of the festival, describing the events that had brought Tenacity to this day and laying out plans for the future. The ground was still too hard for the digging to commence, but it wouldn't be for much longer and then the town could continue looking for more bones. Tiffany looked around. "I really hope they find more dinosaur artifacts. The people of this town deserve something good to happen to them."

"It's going to happen," Ellis said confidently. "And when it does, Tenacity will be famous."

"Fame is not always a good thing."

"You say that as if you have some experience."

"Secondhand. But that's close enough for me. Remember, my sister is married to a huge star. When Stephanie and Geoff were dating, one of his exes gave an interview tearing him down. None of what she said was true, but it didn't stop the celebrity gossip TV shows from airing it or the tabloids from printing dozens of articles about it. My sister was hurt. So was Geoff. And it was all so unnecessary. I suppose that's a by-product of fame."

"I'm sorry that happened to them. But there's a big difference between a town being famous and individuals being famous."

"Maybe. But trust me, there's always a jerk somewhere who'll try to gum up the works. An opportunist who'll try to take advantage of the situation. I hope that doesn't happen in Tenacity."

"It sounds as if the town is starting to grow on you," he said softly. He glanced at her, his brown eyes filled with warmth.

"Does it now?"

"Yes. And just because Dinosaur Days will be ending doesn't mean you have to leave town right away."

"I'm leaving, but my reason has nothing to do with Dinosaur Days. I have a business to run. The only reason I was able to come here at all is because I needed to close my shop while I had some renovations done. When the contractor finishes, I'll be back at work. I have bills to pay as do my employees."

"I see." He walked in silence for a couple of moments and she wondered what he was thinking about. She had a sneaking suspicion it wasn't about the juggler they had just passed. "Just because you're leaving town doesn't mean that our relationship has to come to a screeching halt."

"Relationship? I thought we agreed that we were just friends."

"*Friends who kiss.* Although I have to confess to being disappointed that you haven't given me the signal."

"I'll work on that."

"I'd appreciate it. The sooner the better." He flashed her a wicked grin before getting serious again. "A casual relationship is still a relationship. It just means that we aren't planning to fall in love and get married. I like you and you like me so there's no reason we should stop seeing each other. After all, Tenacity and Bronco aren't that far apart." The idea of continuing to see Ellis was enticing. She hadn't had this much fun with a man in years. Despite their obvious differences, they clicked. But they *were* different. Their differences didn't matter now, but eventually they would grow in importance. The more time she and Ellis spent together, the more things they shared, the closer they would become. And when their differences began to matter—and they inevitably would begin to matter—the fun they shared would diminish. Tiffany didn't see the sense of putting herself in a situation that she knew would end in heartache.

"It's not the physical distance. An hour and a half isn't insurmountable. But there are other considerations. I don't have a nine to five job. Neither do you for that matter. But you have your family to lean on. I'm a sole proprietor. I have a couple of employees, but the responsibility for keeping my business in the black rests solely on my shoulders. That takes hard work and energy. It doesn't leave me a whole lot of free time. And I don't think I'll have enough time to maintain a relationship—even a casual one."

"It wouldn't be easy, but we could make it work."

"Maybe. But there are still our other differences to consider."

"You're only looking at things one way."

"With eyes wide open? Realistically? If there is another way to view things, please tell me." Though Tiffany didn't want to admit it, she hoped Ellis would come up with a convincing argument for them to keep seeing each other.

"Our differences mean that we'll never get bored."

"But they could also keep us from agreeing. Nobody could be happy living in a state of constant battle."

"People compromise."

"Neither one of us would be happy making too many concessions."

"I think we're more alike than you think."

"Really, country boy?"

"Yes. And for a city girl, you look mighty comfortable in those boots and that hat."

After they'd finished with the kids, Tiffany had taken off her headband and put on the Stetson. "These are borrowed. And they're going right back to their owner as soon as I get back to the inn. But anyway, tell me how alike we are."

He smiled. "I'm not going to tell you. I'm going to show you."

"How?"

"I'll go to an event of your choosing and you do something that I pick. If we both enjoy ourselves, we'll keep this..." He waved his hand between them.

"Friends-who-kiss thing?"

"Yes. We'll keep it going."

"What are you going to choose?" she asked warily. What did country folks do for fun? Immediately fishing and hunting ran through her mind. She couldn't imagine having fun doing either of those things.

"Something fun." He removed his cowboy hat, giving her an unobstructed view of his handsome face while he rubbed his forehead with a forearm. Then he set the hat back on his head. "Have you ever gone on a trail ride? On a working ranch—not a ride for tourists."

She shook her head. "No."

"Does it scream *boring*? I don't want to bore you. But if you say yes, you'll get to see my family's ranch."

"You've told me so much about the ranch. I would like to see it."

"Then it's a date. Now, what do you want me to do with you? Go to a spa? Get a facial and a mani-pedi?" Though he was obviously teasing, she heard a hint of horror in his voice that tempted her to say yes, if only to drive home how different they truly were. But that wouldn't have been fair. None of the guys she'd dated had gone to a spa with her. Nor did she want them to. Couples spa days didn't interest her.

"No. But there is a concert I want to attend Saturday after next. Would you like to go with me? Geoff and Stephanie will be finished with their commitments here and we'll all be back home in Bronco by then."

"Sure. I love music. I'm actually a fairly good singer."

She remembered. His voice had done a number on her not too long ago. Just the memory made her knees wobble. "Good. The concert is in Bronco. I already have tickets. I was supposed to go with a friend but she needed to cancel."

"Lucky me. I'll pay for the tickets."

"Don't go all caveman on me. I invited you, remember?"

"At my suggestion."

"Fine. We'll go Dutch."

He heaved out a long breath and then nodded. "Who's playing?"

She named two up and coming neo soul acts.

"I'm not familiar with their music."

"They're independent. You can still back out."

"No way. There's no way I want to miss it. We're going to have a good time."

"I'm sure we will," Tiffany said.

Though she'd spoken calmly, Tiffany couldn't stem the tide of excitement building inside her. She wondered if being this excited was a good thing?

Ellis took Tiffany to the inn and then drove back home. He hadn't expected to enjoy today as much as he had. Dinosaur Days were important to the town and he'd hoped to lead the way as mayor. Losing the election had knocked him off his center, sending him into a tailspin. It had taken him months to find his footing again. Though he still wanted to do more than ranch in his life, he had to admit that he was content for now. He had no doubt that when opportunity knocked—whatever it would be—he would be ready to take a chance again. But for now, life was good and he didn't want to change a thing.

Hanging out with Tiffany today had been great. Even though he hadn't planned on spending the entire day in her booth, he hadn't been able to tear himself away. From the first moment to the last, she'd been positively enchanting. Whenever they'd been close, the warmth radiating from her body had wrapped around him, working its way inside his chest, pushing against his barriers and touching his heart. Every time she smiled at him, heat grew low in his stomach and it had taken supreme effort to douse it. There was no doubt that he was attracted to her. But then, as sexy as she was, especially in those jeans that fit her like a glove, any man would be.

Ellis knew that he needed to be careful. Tiffany had been clear that she didn't want a serious relationship with him. Honestly, he wasn't looking for a romantic entanglement right now either. But his heart seemed to have other ideas. Ideas that should have him rethinking the plan to see more of her.

In the past, he'd had no trouble walking away from a woman when the relationship had run its course. When the woman had chosen to call it quits, he'd wished her well and let her go with a smile on his face. His ego may have taken a hit, but his heart had remained intact. But for some reason it was different with Tiffany. Deep down he knew he wouldn't be able to let Tiffany exit his life without trying to convince her to stay.

Did that mean he wanted a serious relationship? A permanent relationship? Not even close. Sure, he believed in true and lasting love. His parents had been married for more than thirty years, and both sets of grandparents had been married for over fifty. And they were all still deliriously happy after all those years together. If that wasn't proof that love could last, he didn't know what was. But right now he wasn't looking for forever. Or even for a long time. He knew those marriages had required each partner to make dozens, if not hundreds, of big and small compromises over the years. Tiffany had made it clear that, to her, *compromise* was a bad word.

Or had she? He searched his mind, reaching for that particular snippet of conversation so he could replay it. No, she wasn't opposed to compromising. She just didn't want to compromise on something that would change who she authentically was. But most compromises wouldn't require that of her.

Despite their differences, they shared common values. The most important was their belief in being there for their families. Tiffany was in Tenacity because her sister needed help. Sure, the timing had been convenient, but Ellis believed that she would have come to Stephanie's aid even if it hadn't been. Just as he would drop everything if one of his siblings needed him.

Speak of the devil.

He was parking his pickup in his driveway when he spotted the headlights of Tristan's truck behind him. He got out and waited for his brother to join him.

"Did we have plans?" Ellis asked as his brother approached.

"No. But since when do we need to schedule time to get together?"

"True." They went inside Ellis's house and headed straight to the kitchen. Ellis grabbed two beers from the fridge and handed one bottle to his brother. Without saying a word, they headed for the den. When they were each seated in a leather recliner, their feet up, Ellis turned to his brother. "So, what's up?"

Tristan took a swig of his beer before replying. "Just checking to see how things went with you and your new girlfriend. From what I hear, you spent the entire day with her. First in her booth and then walking around the festival."

"How do you know all of this? I didn't see you once today."

"You know how. Nothing in this town happens in secret. Especially when it involves a new romance."

"Whoa. There's no romance. We're just hanging out. Having fun." Of course, it would have been more fun if she'd given him the kissing signal. And maybe she would have if her sister and brother-in-law hadn't arrived at the inn at the same time they had. Geoff had insisted on helping Ellis with Tiffany's boxes. Then Geoff and Stephanie had lingered so they could talk to him and get to know him better. When it became clear to Ellis that he wasn't going to have time alone with Tiffany, he'd said good-night.

"Now that Shane has fallen in love with Remi, the town expects the rest of us Corey brothers to fall like dominoes. As the next oldest, you're next in line. Everyone is watching to see what you do. I wouldn't be surprised if they're taking bets on when you're going to make it official."

"They're going to be watching and waiting for a long time if they expect me to get married. I'm not in the market for a wife. I just happen to enjoy Tiffany's company," Ellis said firmly, quieting the voice that wondered whether that statement was still entirely true.

"Hey," Tristan said, holding his hands in front of him, "don't shoot the messenger. I'm just letting you know what people are saying. And you know some of that talk is going to reach Mom if it hasn't already. Forewarned is forearmed. If you don't want to add kindling to the fire, perhaps you should stop seeing her."

"No way." Ellis's reply came quickly. Perhaps too quickly.

Tristan gave Ellis a knowing look while nodding slowly. "So it's like that, is it?"

Ellis should have known his brother would pounce on his answer and misinterpret it. He should have played it cooler. "It's not *any* way. I just don't let people tell me who I can and can't spend time with."

"Sure. I remember when Shane said something similar. You see how that turned out. Now he's engaged and walking around with a sappy grin on his face. That could be you."

"I thought you were only the messenger. It sounds to me like you've taken a side. And it's not mine."

"Not me. I'm next in line. I want you to hold out as long as you can to keep the pressure off me."

"It's good to know you have my best interests in mind," Ellis said drily and they both laughed.

After that the conversation turned to the upcoming rodeo. Tiffany and Ellis had agreed to go together, something he chose not to share with his brother. Although Tristan claimed to be the messenger, Ellis knew he was also on a fact-finding mission, gathering information to report back to the rest of the family. Ellis wasn't going to give him a scoop.

Besides, there wasn't much to tell about his relationship with Tiffany.

Or was there?

Chapter Six

"Park wherever you can find a spot," Tiffany said to Ellis as they pulled into the Bronco Convention Center parking lot. Located on the outskirts of town, the convention center hosted everything from rodeos to trade shows to exhibitions. Tonight it was the location for an R & B concert. Two of Tiffany's favorite acts would be performing. She danced in her seat in anticipation. Though she'd been disappointed when her friend Lisa needed to cancel, Tiffany had to admit that being here with Ellis was an unexpected pleasure.

Ellis glanced over at her, amusement in his eyes. "And here I was planning to just leave the car in the middle of the road and get out."

"Sorry. I'm just excited."

"I can tell. But this isn't my first rodeo."

"The rodeo was more than a week ago," Tiffany said with a grin. The event had been sold out which given the list of stars competing was no surprise. Geoff and The Hawkins Sisters drew crowds everywhere they went.

"Yes. And I have to say I enjoyed myself immensely. Of course, I always do. There's something about watching man and beast compete with and against each other that gets my blood pumping. And Geoff was outstanding, as usual. He never ceases to amaze with his skill."

"Did you ever think about competing in rodeo?"

"No. Football was always my sport. I started in Pop Warner. I also played on my high school team. Three years varsity. I was first string in my junior and senior years. Now I'm reduced to playing touch with my brothers and our friends. I'm definitely not in the shape I was fifteen years ago."

Tiffany interpreted that comment as an invitation to study his body so she took it. Ellis was dressed in dark blue jeans and a navy and green striped shirt. She didn't have to work hard to see the outline of his muscles under his clothes. They were so big and well defined that they would be visible beneath a parka. If this was out of shape, then she could only imagine what he'd looked like back then. She sighed as she tore her eyes away from his body. She needed to be careful or her lust would get the better of her. "What position did you play?"

"Linebacker." He backed the pickup into a spot and turned off the motor.

"Did you score a lot of touchdowns?"

"No. But then a linebacker plays on the defensive side of the ball. Defensive linemen are more likely to force fumbles than to get an interception." He looked at her. "And you have no clue what I'm talking about."

"I've heard my brothers say those words once or twice in my life. Of course, I was generally running away from the TV as fast as I could at the time so..."

He laughed.

"I'm not big on sports," she admitted. "The only reason I watch rodeo is because of Geoff and the Hawkins Sisters."

"Peeking through your fingers and asking, 'is it over yet' isn't exactly *watching.* Lucky for us, love of sports isn't a requirement to be friends who kiss."

There he went again. Trying to convince her that their differences didn't matter. "There hasn't been much kissing," she grumbled. When she realized that she'd spoken out loud, she wanted to melt into the leather seat. "Forget I said that."

"You're the one in charge of the sign, not me. I'm ready, willing and able. All you have do is give the signal and I'll take it from there."

She wanted to give him the signal then and there, but she held back. Given the strength of the desire coursing through her body right now, one kiss might lead to another two or three. And since she was past the age of wanting to make out in a truck, she ignored her need. "Be on the lookout."

"I always am." His voice was one hundred percent serious and Tiffany shivered. Maybe she had been too hasty when she'd dismissed making out in a truck. Before she could give him the sign, he nudged her shoulder. "Come on. We need to get going or we'll get stuck in line."

They got out of his truck, walked across the rapidly filling lot and got in line. Ellis took her hand and she looked up at him. "We don't want to get separated."

"Okay." Tiffany could have pointed out that the likelihood of that happening was slim to none, but she didn't. She liked the feel of her hand in his. His palm was rough but his touch was gentle. And warm. This was the time of year where Montana weather was ever changing. One day it was sunny and pleasant, perfect for spending time outside. The next, it was cold with wind gusts strong enough to send even the stoutest person scurrying inside. This evening was closer to the latter than the former and Tiffany appreciated the heat that his touch generated.

Ellis rubbed the back of her hand with his thumb. Suddenly, more than her hand was warm. Heat spread throughout her body and she felt tingly all over. This reaction was entirely over the top. It wasn't as if she hadn't held a man's hand before. She'd done that and more. So why was her body behaving as if she was some blushing virgin on her wedding night? She had no idea, but she wished her body would knock it off. She and Ellis weren't romantically involved and they certainly weren't going to get married. It was past time for her rebellious body to get with the program.

When they reached the front of the line, Tiffany held up her phone, showing their tickets to the usher who waved them inside, then directed them to their main floor seats. When they reached their row, Tiffany took off her leather jacket and then glanced over at Ellis. He was staring at her, appreciation in his eyes. Tiffany had dressed with extra care tonight, putting on a thin purple sweater that stopped at her waist and tight black jeans. Black thigh-high boots with four-inch heels and silver jewelry completed the look. Though she generally applied her makeup with a light hand, choosing subtle shades that blended with her natural coloring, tonight she wore bright red lipstick and lots of eye shadow and mascara. She enjoyed dressing up and looking her best, and tonight Ellis's attention told her he appreciated it, too.

"I know I said it before, Tiffany, but it bears repeating. You look sensational." Ellis's voice was husky and Tiffany's heart skipped a beat.

"Thanks. You don't look too shabby yourself."

He flashed her a wide smile that made her briefly consider the possibility of having a relationship with him. At least for the night.

The arena was noisy, so Tiffany and Ellis had to lean in close in order to continue their conversation. His masculine scent teased her, putting her nerve endings on high alert. Every time his hard shoulder brushed against hers, she felt a jolt of electricity. When the din grew too loud for them to talk without yelling, they gave up and sat in comfortable silence. Tiffany sneaked a peek at Ellis who appeared totally relaxed. Clearly he was as content to be quiet as he was making conversation.

That was one thing that she was coming to learn about him. Ellis was at ease in his skin and he didn't feel the need to pretend to be something that he wasn't. After dealing with an ex who'd lied as easily and as naturally as he breathed, changing his personality as the situation required, that was refreshing.

After her troubles with her lying ex, Tiffany had given online dating a try. It hadn't taken long for her to discover that those men had also been given to exaggeration and deception, if not to the same extent. It hadn't taken long for her to decide that online dating wasn't for her. But since she hadn't personally met any man who interested her, that didn't leave many options.

The lights in the arena dimmed and Ellis and Tiffany shared a smile before turning their attention to the stage. Red and blue lights moved across the stage before settling on the drummer who played a long drumroll. Then the first strains of a popular song began to play. White lights illuminated the singers and as one, the audience members rose to their feet and began to clap and dance to the music.

Tiffany glanced out of the corner of her eye at Ellis. He had also risen and was clapping along. The band played two more up-tempo songs before slowing things down and playing a sweet ballad and they sat back down.

The group sang several more songs and one from their newest release before ending their show with their biggest hit. Then the lights came up as there was a brief intermission between acts.

"I hope you're having a good time. Concerts are more fun when you're familiar with the music," Tiffany said as they stood in line for concessions.

"I'm having a great time. I don't know the songs, but the musicians are great. It makes me remember how much I enjoy concerts. It's been a long time since I've been to one."

"Really?" Tiffany said. "I go to concerts every chance I get."

"I wonder why I haven't done this more often. I suppose living in a struggling small town doesn't help. Not too many big acts come to Tenacity."

"Believe it or not, Bronco doesn't usually make the cut when the biggest artists are putting their tours together. I've had to travel to see my favorites. I also love musicals and live theater. In the past, I even hopped on a plane and gone to New York and Chicago to see a show. Of course, now that I have my business, I've had to cut back on travel. I don't have that kind of time—or money—for those extravagances. I have to watch my pennies now."

He laughed. "In that case, your snacks are on me."

Tiffany sputtered. "That wasn't a hint."

"You think I don't know that? I was going to offer to buy whatever you wanted anyway. Now I'm going to insist."

"Well, then." Tiffany said, "I guess you told me."

"Lucky for you, I'm a big saver. I've always believed that it's easier to save a dollar than it is to work to replace it."

"There's some truth in that. But I'd rather have experiences than a bank account with a lot of zeros."

"Why not both?"

"I didn't know that was an option. Where do I sign up?"

Ellis laughed. They reached the front of the line and ordered their snacks. They were just returning to their seats when the headliners took the stage. This group was one of Tiffany's bucket-list acts and they didn't disappoint. They put on quite a show, playing all of her favorite songs. By the time they'd completed their third encore and left the stage for the final time, Tiffany was hoarse from cheering.

"Best concert ever," she said to Ellis when the lights came up.

"You'll get no argument from me. In fact, I'm already wondering who's going on tour next."

"Uh-oh. I think I may have created a monster."

Ellis laughed and then helped Tiffany put on her jacket. His hands lingered on her shoulders and Tiffany felt a sudden rush of desire. The warmth from his body surrounded her and she was tempted to lean her head against his firm chest. And then what? They were in a crowded auditorium. People didn't appear to be paying attention to them, but they weren't doing anything to attract attention. But indulging in a hot kiss could cause someone to pull out a phone and shoot a video. One impetuous moment could live forever on the internet. As a business owner, her public image mattered. Any negative publicity could affect her bottom line, so she tamped down her lust and walked beside Ellis through the convention center and back to his truck.

When they were inside, he turned to her. "I don't know about you, but I'm hungry."

"Of course you are. You're always hungry."

He laughed. "I'm a growing boy. Is there anywhere still open where we can get something to eat?"

"Plenty of places. Remember, you're not in Tenacity anymore. The sidewalks don't roll up at nine. What do you have a taste for?"

"Anything. As long as it's good."

She thought for a moment. “Let’s go to DJ’s Deluxe. I know you like ribs.”

“That sounds good. Just tell me how to get there.”

Tiffany gave the directions and before long they were being seated at a booth near the front of the restaurant.

“This is a nice place,” Ellis said, his gaze encompassing the dining room’s elaborate decor. “Definitely different from ribs on a blanket in the park.”

“Don’t sell that day short,” Tiffany said. “I had a good time. Besides, differences are good. As the saying goes, variety is the spice of life. I for one like to have a variety of experiences.”

Ellis gave her a sharp look and she realized that he’d been saying the same thing for days. Luckily he didn’t point out that fact.

After they perused the menu, they placed their order with the waiter who immediately returned with their drinks. Ellis took a swallow of his beer and leaned against the back of the booth. “Did you grow up in Bronco?”

“Yes. In Bronco Valley. I have an apartment in Bronco Heights now.”

“I thought the name of the town was Bronco.”

“It has two sides, for lack of a better term. Bronco Heights is where the wealthier people live—although I’m not wealthy by any stretch of the imagination—and Bronco Valley is where the working and middle class families live. My parents still live in the same house where I grew up.”

“How many kids are there in your family?”

“There are five of us. Brittany is the oldest. She’s

married to a rancher and has two sweet kids. I also have two brothers, Ethan and Lucas. And you already met Stephanie. We're all very close and I count my siblings among my best friends. My parents own a string of dry cleaners so they work a lot. They taught us that you have to work for what you want. They're supportive of us and our dreams but they're also no-nonsense types."

"It sounds as if your childhood was similar to mine."

Tiffany folded her arms across her chest. "I know you aren't going to tell me that growing up on a ranch is just like growing up in Bronco. I don't see how that can even remotely be true."

"Maybe not the setting. But we were both raised by parents who taught us the importance of hard work. They also stressed the importance of family, which is why we're so close to our siblings. That's more important than where we were raised."

"What is it with you trying to convince me that our differences don't matter? I thought you weren't interested in a serious relationship."

He held up his hands as if warding off evil. "That hasn't changed. Believe me, I'm not looking for anything approaching serious."

"Then what's this all about?"

He frowned. "I suppose I'm trying to get you to see that Bronco and Tenacity aren't that different."

Tiffany sighed, trying to come up with the right words. "Tenacity *is* different from Bronco. There's no denying that. Tenacity is scraping by while Bronco is prosperous with plenty going for it."

"Fair enough. But Tenacity will be prosperous soon, You'll see."

Tiffany only nodded. Hopefully things would work out the way he hoped.

At that moment, the waiter brought their plates of ribs and set them on the table. "Wait until you taste these. Your tastebuds will never be the same."

After making sure that Tiffany and Ellis had everything they needed, the waiter told them to enjoy their meals and stepped away.

"Smells good," Ellis said.

"They taste even better," Tiffany said.

Ellis nodded, then picked up a juicy rib and took a big bite.

"What do you think?" Tiffany asked, taking a bite of one of her own. She smothered a groan of pleasure.

"Delicious. They're almost as good as the ones that the Grizzly Bar serves."

Tiffany laughed. "And here I was thinking that those ribs were nearly as good as these."

"The only thing that is missing is my grandmother's mac and cheese. She makes the best in Tenacity. Just ask anyone."

"Mac and cheese would be perfect right now," Tiffany agreed. "But the fries aren't bad."

As she and Ellis ate their meals, Tiffany found herself completely relaxed. She was having more fun than she'd had in a long time. Given her reluctance to risk her heart, that wasn't a good thing.

"This scar comes from the time my older brother, Shane, dared me to walk the fence post with my eyes closed," Ellis said, pointing to a place on his eyebrow where the hair was missing. The scar was tiny, but given how close it was to his eye, it could have been catastrophic, as his mother had pointed out countless times over the years.

"And you did it." That statement held more than a little bit of shock. Tiffany clucked her tongue in obvious disapproval.

"Of course I did. There was no way my pride would allow me to back away from a challenge. Especially since my other brothers were watching to see if I was going to chicken out."

"How old were you?"

"Ten. But my age had nothing to do with anything. I would have done it at twelve or fifteen. Heck, if he dared me today and Tristan and Aaron were standing around watching, I would probably do it."

Her laughter was a sweet sound that awakened a desire in him that was growing stronger by the moment. She shook her head and her shiny hair brushed against her shoulders. His hands ached to touch those strands to see if they were as soft as they looked.

"I can't believe that even at your big old age you still haven't learned that it's okay to walk away from a dare. Wiser even."

"Would it make a difference if I told you that he double-dog dared me?"

"Let me think." She pursed her full lips and he imagined how good it would feel to kiss her again. Even now, he hadn't been able to forget how it had felt to kiss her. The memory popped into his mind at the most inconvenient times. Just yesterday he'd barely managed to keep his hold on a steer that he was helping his brothers tag. Shane had read him the riot act. Ellis hadn't said a word in his defense because he knew he'd deserved it. He really needed Tiffany to give him the sign. And soon. "I'm going to have to go with a no."

"That's because you're a woman. If you were a man you would totally understand."

"Because as a woman I have better sense than to let my pride get me into trouble." She paused and an odd look flashed across her face. Then she blinked and it was gone. "At least I hope that's the case."

"There's only one way to find out." He grinned and leaned close to her and was extremely pleased when she leaned in, too. "I dare you to kiss me. Right here in this restaurant."

"Or what?"

"What do you mean *or what*? That's the dare."

"That's not much of a dare." She dabbed her napkin against her lips, removing a bit of barbecue sauce, then pecked him on his mouth. Without missing a beat, she picked up a fry, swirled it in ketchup and popped it into her mouth. Momentarily distracted by how sensuous she looked when she chewed, he didn't point out that that half second contact barely qualified as a kiss. At least not the kind he'd envisioned.

"I guess I should have dared you to do something else. But I win. I proved my point."

"What point would that be?"

"You didn't walk away from the challenge. So that

proves that my not walking away from a double-dog dare was reasonable. Necessary even."

"Or it could show that I wanted to kiss you and you gave me the perfect opportunity to do so."

He was picking up a rib when the full import of her words hit him. Suddenly his fingers grew limp and the meat dropped back onto his plate. Shocked, he could only stare at her. Then he grinned. "Is that right?"

"It's a possibility. Of course, there are numerous others that we could consider."

"How about we stick with that one and let me have another win?"

"You can't get the win both ways. Either you win because I gave into the dare or you win because I wanted to kiss you."

"That's where you're wrong. I wanted you to kiss me regardless of your reason."

"Is that right?"

He nodded. "That's right."

"You didn't have to go through all that trouble. You could have just asked."

"Maybe. But daring you added to the fun."

"I'll have to test that theory."

"Any time you're ready." Ellis said. "Do you want to dare me to kiss you? Because the kiss I'll give you will curl your toes and set you on fire from head to toe."

"Really?" She gave him a devilish grin and leaned her chin into her hand.

"Definitely," he said, moving in closer. Their lips were mere centimeters apart. It wouldn't take much to close the distance.

She laughed and sat up straight, leaving him disappointed. "Sorry, no. I have something else in mind."

"Just as long as it's not too far-fetched."

"Like what? Walk blindfolded across a fence rail? Something you just admitted you would do again today. Don't worry, spending the night in the emergency room is not my idea of a good time."

"What is your idea of a good time?"

"Not that."

"I'm serious. I know you like concerts. What else do you like?"

"I like walking on the beach barefoot. That's one of my most favorite things to do. I love the feel of sand between my toes."

"There aren't many sandy beaches around here. Or does Bronco have one that I'm not aware of?"

"We take it up in the winter," she said drily. "I also love a spirited conversation."

"Is that code for arguing?"

She rolled her eyes. "You sound just like my brothers."

Yikes! They'd ruled out a long-term relationship, but that didn't mean he wanted her to think of him as her brother. That was even worse than being friend-zoned.

Despite their understanding, he was attracted to her. She was the most beautiful woman he'd ever seen. Every inch of her slender body exuded sex appeal. He thought she'd shared the attraction but had decided to ignore it. He'd caught her looking at him when she didn't think he was aware. Call him vain, but whenever he'd felt her eyes on him, he'd flexed his muscles hoping to impress her.

And she just compared him to her brothers!

"Maybe it's a man thing." He hoped.

"No, I've heard it from women, too."

"Ah, then perhaps there's some truth to it. Maybe you do enjoy arguing."

She shrugged, and his eyes were immediately drawn to her perky breasts. "It's the simple things in life, you know?"

He was getting warm and he needed to regain control before he embarrassed himself. "So I've been told. I didn't think that arguing was among them. Anyway, what else do you enjoy?"

"The usual. Spa days. I love a mani-pedi. And I never miss my monthly facial."

"Your skin is beautiful," he said before he could stop himself. But then, it was true. And he didn't believe in holding back compliments. Any opportunity he had to make a person feel better, he took it.

"Thanks." She gave him a look. "Now we've gone over what I like. What do you like to do?"

He thought for a moment. None of his pastimes compared to what she did for entertainment. He'd never flown to New York or Chicago in order to see a play, nor had he traveled out of town just to see a concert. The thought had never occurred to him. His life was small in comparison to hers. And boring. Nevertheless, he would answer as honestly as he could and hope that she was as impressed by him as he was by her.

"I like spending time on the ranch. I have my own

house there," he reminded her, just in case she forgot. He didn't want her to think that he still lived with his parents at thirty-three. "I love my family but I need my privacy."

"You don't have to explain it to me. I know what it's like to have family all up in your business like they're being paid to be there."

"Exactly. When I have time, and the weather is nice, I ride out on the range and camp out alone for a day or so."

"That sounds peaceful."

"It is. But it's definitely not as exciting as jetting off to New York for a Broadway show."

She shrugged. Who knew moving a shoulder could be so sexy? "You have your way of recharging and I have mine. As long as it works, what's the problem?"

"Wait a minute. Are you trying to say that our differences don't matter after all?" He was teasing, but it was fun to watch her squirm.

"I'm not saying that at all. We are different. And if I was looking for a husband, which I am not, I wouldn't be talking to you at all because of those differences. But something short-term with no promises or expectations? Maybe the differences won't matter that much. Remember, we're trying to decide if we can enjoy ourselves doing something the other chooses before we decide whether to continue with our arrangement."

He was trying to think of a suitable reply when their waiter stepped up to the table. "Would either of you like another beer?"

Ellis sighed. "I would like one, but I have a long drive ahead of me. But I will take another glass of water."

"Wait a minute," Tiffany said to the waiter and then turned to Ellis. "Go ahead and get the beer."

"I really shouldn't. The drive—"

"You don't have to worry about that tonight. You can stay with me."

Ellis looked at her, wanting to be sure that he understood her meaning.

Tiffany met his gaze and lifted the corner of her mouth. "I've come up with my dare, Ellis. That is, if you think you can handle it."

"I can." His heart thumped in anticipation, but he knew he had to bide his time. No woman found desperation attractive. He turned to the waiter. "I'd like that beer after all. And the check."

When the waiter walked away, Ellis turned back to Tiffany. He touched her hand. "Are you sure about this?"

"Positive. I like you and you like me. Neither one of us is looking to turn this—" she waved her hand between the two of them "—into something that it's not. It's not the next great romance or anything close to that. But that doesn't mean we can't enjoy each other's company."

"So, let me be clear. We've agreed that our relationship isn't a permanent one. Is it exclusive?"

"I would prefer it that way." Her eyes clouded over and he had the feeling that expression hid a multitude of emotions and possibly heartache. But he wasn't going to ask her about it. She'd been clear that he was not the type of man she'd choose to be with permanently, so obviously she wouldn't want to share her deepest thoughts with him.

"So would I. I've never dated more than one woman at a time. I never wanted to. I don't have a lot of free time. Dividing it between multiple women would be a mess. In the end, nobody would be happy. Worse, someone could be hurt. So even though our relationship comes with an expiration date, it will be just you and me. Now about that dare…?"

Chapter Seven

"Come on in," Tiffany said as she opened the door to her apartment and stepped inside. She turned on a lamp in the small entry, chasing away the darkness. Even with the light, the space felt intimate. She took a seat on a padded bench, pulled off her shoes and slipped on house shoes. They were pink and girly and fit Tiffany perfectly.

"Thanks." Ellis sat beside Tiffany and toed off his boots, set them next to the bench, then followed her into the front room. The drapes were open, revealing the full moon and the starry sky. The silhouette of the mountains was visible in the distance. He whistled as he walked closer and peered out the window. "This must be some view in the daytime."

"It is. This sight always relaxes me and starts my day off right. I mean, how can you stress over anything when this majestic sight is right outside your front window?"

"It's nice. But I have to tell you that the view on my family's ranch is pretty spectacular, too."

She nodded. "I'll take your word for it."

"You don't have to. Remember, you're going riding with me. You'll have the chance to see for yourself."

"That's true."

Ellis took one last glance out the window and turned back to Tiffany's apartment. It was beautifully decorated. Not that he expected anything less from someone as elegant as she was. The colors were warm and the fabrics were soft. A large framed painting of a sandy beach hung over the couch. There were floral pillows on the chairs and vases of fresh flowers on the tables. Evidence that a woman lived here. Though the decor was completely different than his, he still felt comfortable.

"Have a seat," Tiffany said. "Would you like a drink? I think I have beer. Or would you prefer a glass of wine?"

Ellis grinned. "If I didn't know better, I'd think that you were trying to get me drunk so you could have your way with me."

"The thought never crossed my mind."

"What do I have to do to make it cross your mind and maybe even stay there for a while?"

Tiffany laughed. "You're so funny."

"I suppose you prefer a more serious type of man. The sophisticated kind who never smiles or makes silly jokes." The kind of man he would never be. The kind of man he didn't want to be.

She shook her head. "Not even close. The last thing I want to do is spend time with a stick-in-the-mud. Life is too short to be around someone who bores me within an inch of my life."

"That's good to know," he said with a smile.

"But on the other hand, I don't want a man who always has to be the life of the party either. I like quiet times and quiet conversations, too. All in all, I think you're just right."

He stretched his legs in front of him and crossed them at the ankle. Then he cupped his hands behind his head—the picture of satisfaction. "I'm just right."

"Don't let it go to your head. And don't get too comfortable. There's still the matter of the dare. I might even double-dog dare you."

"Go for it. Do you want to hear me sing?" He sang the first line of a popular song, holding the last note a little longer than necessary as if showing off his great pipes.

"That's not what I was going to dare you to do."

"Maybe you want to see me dance." He jumped to his feet and began to swivel his hips and snap his fingers.

She held up a hand to stop him. "I don't think you understand how dares work. I'm supposed to tell you what I want you to do. You don't get to choose for yourself. Though I do appreciate learning that you have rhythm. I like a man who has the moves."

"Was that ever in doubt?"

"I never make assumptions." She leaned back in her chair and then smiled at him. "But we're getting off track here. If I didn't know better, I would think you were deliberately trying to distract me."

"Not a chance." He bowed at the waist and extended an arm. "The floor is yours, Ms. Brandt. Make your dare."

Instead of answering, she stood up, crossed the room and closed the drapes. "Privacy and all that."

"Okay." He folded his arms and rocked back on his heels, waiting.

"I dare you to take off your shirt." She grinned, then looked into his eyes. He read the challenge there.

"That's not much of a dare, but okay." He slowly undid the buttons, holding her gaze the entire time. Then he slid the fabric from his shoulders. Her eyes traveled over his bare torso and, in that moment, he was so glad for the hours of hard work that ranching required.

"Next, I double-dog dare you to—"

He held up his hand, noticing with no small amount of satisfaction that her eyes darkened as his muscles flexed. This was going to be fun. "Wait a minute. It's my turn to dare you. It's only fair."

"I'm not the one who said that I would accept any dare, anytime."

"I don't recall saying those exact words, but I get your point. It's true that you didn't agree to any more dares. And if you want to back out, I completely understand. It's just that I didn't take you for a chicken, but maybe I was mistaken."

She huffed out a breath, just as he'd expected. Tiffany wasn't the type to walk away from a challenge. "I'm in. Do your best, Cowboy. What do you dare me to do?"

Tiffany knew that Ellis was goading her—his too-innocent expression was a dead giveaway—but even knowing that, she still couldn't say no. Her pride wouldn't let him win. She was going to wipe that satisfied grin off his face.

"I dare you to remove your sweater."

"That's it?" She'd seen that coming. No doubt his challenges would echo hers. She needed to keep that in mind. Not that there was anything she wouldn't do tonight.

"That's it."

Tiffany thought about how Ellis had teased her by undoing each of his buttons painfully slowly. She could have teased him in the same way, but she decided to ramp up the sexual tension that was growing between them. She wanted to make him do more than stare. She wanted to make him sweat.

Tiffany's top only had two buttons near the collar which she unfastened with one hand. Then she grabbed the bottom of her sweater and, in one smooth move, tugged it over her head and then tossed it at Ellis's feet. Grinning, she looked into his face. His eyes were dark and she easily read the lust there. She knew she looked good in her purple lace bra. Though she hadn't known how the evening would end, she'd been hopeful and had dressed for the occasion.

She tossed her hair over her shoulders and struck a pose, pleased when his mouth fell open. "I think it's my turn now. Unless you want to quit."

"Never." That one word, spoken so firmly, sent a shiver down her spine.

She grinned. "Then I dare you to put your shirt back on."

"Really?" Ellis's voice dripped with shock and disappointment.

"No," Tiffany said and then laughed at the utter relief on his face. "I dare you to take off your pants."

"I was hoping you would say that."

Humming "The Stripper" in his deep baritone, Ellis unfastened his belt and pulled it from the loops of his jeans, rocking his hips from side to side in a seductive movement that had Tiffany fanning herself. Grinning broadly, he unfastened the button on his jeans and began walking in her direction. Though he was only goofing around, he was raising her temperature and her mouth began to water. When he was close enough for the heat from his body to reach out and touch her, he unzipped his jeans. Tantalizingly slowly, he slid them down, revealing his muscular thighs and calves. Ellis stepped out of his pants and stood there in gray boxer briefs that left nothing to the imagination. When Tiffany realized that her mouth was hanging open, she snapped it shut. Even so, she couldn't tear her eyes away from his magnificent physique.

"I guess it's my turn," Ellis said.

Tiffany forced herself to meet his gaze. His eyes gleamed with mischief. "I don't know what gave you that idea. We dared each other twice. That should be enough, don't you think?"

His smile faded and he reached for his pants. "If that's what you think. Obviously I'll go along with whatever you want."

"It's not," Tiffany said, unable to hold back her

laughter. "Not even close. I can't believe you fell for that again. Go ahead and dare away."

He gave her a searching look. "Only if you're sure. I don't want to put pressure on you."

"I'm not feeling the slightest bit of pressure. I'm actually having a great time." And she was anticipating having an even better one very shortly.

"In that case, despite how sexy you look in them, I dare you to remove your pants."

Ellis was still standing near her, so as Tiffany shimmied out of her jeans, her legs brushed up against his and her nerves tingled. A groan slipped through his lips and a feeling of triumph surged through her at the sound. When her pants were off and she was only wearing her purple bra and thong, she turned in a slow circle, giving him an unobstructed view of her backside. When she was facing Ellis again, his eyes blazed with desire. Then she took his hand, holding his gaze.

"One last dare," she said, "I dare you to come into my bedroom with me and see what comes next."

His devilish smile was enough to weaken her knees. "It will be my pleasure."

"I'm pretty sure that it will be a pleasure for both of us."

The sunlight streaming through the sheer curtains woke Tiffany and she pulled her pillow over her head, doing her best to block out the light. Last night had been wonderful if exhausting. It had been like something out of a movie and she wanted to bask in the glow for a little while longer. Sadly, she'd never been able to go back to sleep once she'd awakened, so she removed the pillow, stretched and then opened her eyes. Ellis was lying beside her, his arms and legs flung wide. His bare chest rose and fell with each breath he took. Since his eyes were closed in slumber, Tiffany took the quiet moment to study his body. It was exquisite. There wasn't an ounce of fat on him. Every inch of his six feet plus body was pure muscle.

She smiled as she recalled running her hands over his body last night, marveling at how smooth his rich brown skin felt beneath her touch. Ellis had felt just as free to touch her body, caressing every inch of her until she was on fire with desire. He had made her feel things she had never felt before. And not just physically, although the climaxes had been higher and more intense than anything she'd ever known. But the physical pleasure had only been part of the experience. He'd also stirred emotions inside her with an intensity that was entirely new.

Last night, she'd been filled with too much pleasure to care about how easily he'd reached her emotions. How close he'd come to getting inside her heart. But now, in the cold light of day, when she was no longer caught up in the throes of passion, she couldn't help but worry. Was it wise to get so close to Ellis? Didn't she know better than to let her emotions get away from her? Surely she hadn't forgotten the pain of a broken heart. Yet here she was, falling for him. And she didn't want to fall for him. They'd already decided that there was no future for them. Yet she couldn't make herself walk away. She was her happiest when she was around him.

He made her laugh. It had been a long time since a man had made her feel lighthearted enough to do more than smile. Though she longed to experience true joy, she didn't want to experience that joy with him.

But he was here with her now, so she may as well enjoy the view. Her eyes traveled from his feet up to his face, slowing when they reached the most interesting places. When her gaze reached his eyes, she was surprised to see that they were open. Not only that, he was fully aware of the way she'd been studying him. There was no use pretending that she hadn't been lusting after his body. The way they'd made love last night—three earth-shattering times—had removed any doubt about how attracted she was to him. An attraction she knew he shared.

He reached out and caressed her cheek and all of her worries disappeared. "I can't think of a better way to start the day than waking up with a beautiful woman lying in bed next to me."

"Do you do this often?" Tiffany asked, trying to keep her voice light. Doubts tried to worm their way into her mind, but she shoved them away. What difference did it make if he did? This thing between them wasn't destined to become a great romance like her sisters had with their husbands. This was a fling. When she was ready to search for true love, it would be with someone different from Ellis. Okay, not different exactly. She liked Ellis's sense of humor and his honor. She appreciated his kindness and how gentle he'd been last night when they'd made love. The problem wasn't him. The problem was… She couldn't put it into words when he was touching her.

"I know this may be hard to believe, given my charm and good looks," he said with a chuckle before becoming serious, "but hardly ever. I'm in my thirties, so I can't pretend that I haven't been with women before you. But I'm selective. I don't hop into bed with every woman who catches my eye."

Tiffany relaxed. She didn't need his words to make her feel special—she already knew her worth—but they did. Her ego had taken a huge hit by her ex's betrayal. She'd begun to believe that she'd been the one who was lacking. He'd made her feel as if she wasn't woman enough to satisfy a man. He'd told her that it was her inability to keep him happy that had compelled him to become involved with another woman. She'd known intellectually that it was a lame excuse, but a part of her had taken his words to heart and it had taken a lot of work to get over them.

"Same," Tiffany said, bringing her attention back to the man who deserved it. "Not that you asked."

"And I never would." He turned so they were looking directly at each other. "Your past is not my business. There may be a double standard when it comes to women, but not for me."

He was saying all the right things, making himself even more irresistible. If she wasn't certain that they weren't right for each other, she would let herself fall in love with him. But she wasn't ready to risk it all, especially with someone who lived in Tenacity. The town wasn't for her. She didn't want to live there and couldn't ever imagine being happy there. And Ellis would never leave his ranch. In fact, he was so attached to the town that he'd wanted to be the mayor. And she wouldn't leave Tiffany in Bloom, not after pouring her heart and soul into the business. It was too bad, but relationships were hard enough without a huge barrier waiting to pull them in opposite directions. The best thing for both of them was to keep their hearts locked away and separate from this relationship.

"What are you doing today?" Ellis asked, breaking into her thoughts. Since she didn't like where they were leading, she was grateful for the interruption.

She finger-combed her hair, then twisted it on top of her head and tucked it into a bun. "I'm meeting my sisters for a spa day. Why?"

"I thought we could spend more time together."

Despite not wanting to get emotionally involved, Tiffany smiled. She felt the same way. Especially if some of that time was spent here in her bed. "I'm free tomorrow. Would that work with you?"

"Yes. We can go on that trail ride I promised you."

"Oh." Tiffany hesitated. She hadn't been on a horse in her life. She hadn't even been close to one as an adult. When she'd agreed to go on the ride, she hadn't thought the day would actually come. Now it was staring her in the face. Ellis's hopeful smile began to fade and she wondered how he'd interpreted her silence. "Well, to tell you the truth…"

"What? You aren't going to say that now that you've taken advantage of me three times, you want to set me free? I can't believe you were only using me for my body." He closed his eyes, but not before Tiffany saw the disappointment there. He was trying to cover his feelings by making a joke, but she knew she'd hurt him. Her heart sank to her toes. That was the last thing she wanted to do.

"Ellis. What I was going to say is that…" Tiffany took a deep breath and then blurted, "I'm kind of afraid of horses."

His eyes flew open. She thought she might see laughter or even shock. Instead, they were filled with understanding. Kindness. A typical Ellis reaction. "I don't understand. Why didn't you just tell me that when I asked you to go riding?"

"I guess because I felt a little bit foolish. There are a lot of ranches near Bronco. And my brother-in-law is none other than the great Geoff Burris. How can I possibly be afraid of horses?"

"Do you want to go? Because if you don't, there are plenty of other things we can do together. The main thing is that you have fun."

"I want to go. I know it's irrational to be afraid of horses. But I can't help it. They're so big. And their teeth are enormous. If one bites you, it's going to hurt. You know that picture that kids take on the back of a pony? I never took one. My parents tried to put me on the pony for the picture and I pitched the biggest fit of my childhood, which is saying something."

"Wow. Who would have thought that the magnificent Tiffany Brandt would be afraid of horses?"

Wait a minute. Did Ellis just call her magnificent? The walls that she'd erected around her heart were going to come tumbling down around her feet if he kept talking like this. "Maybe afraid is too strong a word. Maybe apprehensive is a better choice."

He laughed. "It's okay, Tiff. Your secret is safe with me. Does anyone call you Tiff?"

"Not if they expect me to answer, *El*."

"Point taken. So, are we going to go riding tomorrow?"

"Yes." Ellis thought she was magnificent so she couldn't back down now. She was going to live up to that description. That meant that she had twenty-four hours to overcome her fear—er, *apprehension*—of horses.

"Great. Then I suppose I should get dressed and get out of your hair. I need to get back to the ranch."

She drew a finger down his chest. "Only if you insist."

Groaning deep in his throat, he grabbed her hand and brought it to his lips. He pressed a lingering kiss on her fingers. "Don't tempt me, Tiffany. Not unless you intend to break your appointment with your sisters."

She was actually considering it. But if she cancelled, there would be questions to answer later. Questions Tiffany wasn't ready to answer. She sighed. "Fine. We both have places to be. Let's just get dressed before I change my mind."

Ellis grinned at the disappointment Tiffany hadn't been able to keep from her voice. "I'm willing to take a raincheck if you're giving them out."

She nodded. She would definitely like a repeat of last night. "I'll see what I can do."

Forcing her eyes from Ellis's body as he pulled on his clothes, Tiffany slipped into a pink silk robe. Unwilling or unable to stop touching each other, they held hands as they walked through her apartment. When they reached her front door, Ellis pulled Tiffany into a tight embrace. Then he brushed his lips across hers in a gentle kiss that was powerful enough to weaken her knees. "Have fun with your sisters. I'll pick you up tomorrow at ten."

"I'll be waiting."

After Ellis left, Tiffany leaned against the closed door and slowly slid down it until she was sitting on the floor. *Wow.* She tried to find words to describe how she was feeling, but there were too many emotions battling for dominance for her to settle on just one. Suffice it to say she was shook. She glanced at the clock on the table and forced herself to stand. Though she wanted to relive every blissful moment of last night, if she didn't get up now, she would be late.

Tiffany took a shower, pulled her hair into a ponytail and got dressed in under fifteen minutes. Her sisters were getting out of their cars when she pulled into the parking lot of the Bronco Day Spa with two minutes to spare. The three of them hugged before stepping inside the elegantly decorated waiting room. They checked in for their appointments and then sat down in comfortable chairs.

"You look happy," Stephanie said, looking at Tiffany. There was a tone in her sister's voice that Tiffany recognized and she had to stop herself from cringing.

Stephanie had always been able to see what Tiffany tried to hide.

"I'm always happy," Tiffany said. She tried to contain her smile, but she couldn't quite pull it off.

"Maybe," Stephanie said slowly, "but this is different."

"You're glowing," Brittany said. Then she pursed her lips and stared at Tiffany who struggled not to squirm. "What did you do last night?"

Tiffany felt her face get warm and it took everything inside her to not clap her hands on her cheeks. There was no way that her sisters could tell that she spent the night in Ellis's arms just by looking at her. "I went to that concert. Remember? I told you about it."

"Who did you go with?" Brittany asked.

"I bet I know," Stephanie said. "You went with Ellis."

"Who's Ellis?" Brittany asked. "When did you start seeing him? And why am I the last to know?"

"Ellis is a man I met while I was in Tenacity with Stephanie and Geoff. And I'm not *seeing* him, at least not in the way you mean. We're friends." *Friends who kiss and more.* "And yes, we went to the concert together."

"I can bet where you went next," Stephanie said, a knowing grin on her face.

"Yes, to DJ's Deluxe."

"That was smart," Brittany added. "You had to feed him so he'd have enough energy to survive the night."

"I'm not going to dignify that remark with a reply," Tiffany said, turning up her nose.

"There's no need," Stephanie said. "We already have everything we need to know."

"I don't. I need to know more," Brittany said. "But first and most importantly—did you have a good time?"

Tiffany sighed and gave up all pretense of being indifferent. Her sisters weren't falling for it anyway. "The best."

"That's what matters," Brittany said and Stephanie nodded in agreement. "Now, are you serious about him?"

"No. You know I don't do serious relationships."

Brittany took Tiffany's hand and slipped into big sister mode. When she spoke, her voice was gentle. "Don't say that. We all know what that snake did. How he lied and cheated on you. But that just means he isn't deserving of love. You are."

"I know that. But I'm having a good time playing the field."

"Playing the field?" Brittany scoffed. "You aren't anywhere near the field. Ellis is the first man that you've even talked to in over a year."

"I'm picky," Tiffany said, hoping that answer would satisfy her sisters.

"That's good. You should be," Stephanie said. "Does Ellis meet your standards?"

Tiffany nodded. "He totally does. He's charming and smart and has a kind heart. He genuinely cares about other people. And he's also easy on the eyes. Not that his looks are all that important."

"They matter," Brittany said with a grin. "Think of the children."

"You are so bad," Tiffany said and the three of them laughed.

"So are you going to see him again?" Stephanie asked after their laughter died down.

"Tomorrow. We're going to go horseback riding on his ranch."

"You? On a horse?" Brittany asked. "You must really like this guy."

"He's okay," Tiffany said quickly, not meeting her sister's gaze.

"Tiffany, it's okay. You can admit that you like him. The world won't end if you fall in love," Brittany said.

"Wait a minute," Tiffany said, fighting back panic. "Who said anything about falling in love? We just met. I can literally count on one hand the number of dates we've gone on."

"Please do," Brittany said. "I need to catch up."

Stephanie spoke up before Tiffany could reply. "I know that you met at the park for lunch. And the concert. That makes two."

"Don't forget the night in heaven," Brittany teased, singing the last word. "That should get its own category."

"And that is the sum total of our dates," Tiffany said, leaving out their lunch at Castillo's Mexican Restaurant. She didn't want to add fuel to her sisters' fire. "Even though we're going to spend the day together tomorrow, that's still not enough time to fall in love. And it's certainly not enough time to talk about a future."

"I don't know about that. Brittany and Daniel got

married pretty quickly after they met," Stephanie pointed out.

"But that was all pretend so he could maintain custody of his infant niece," Tiffany pointed out. "So I'm not sure that it counts. Have we forgiven you for deceiving us?"

"Considering that it was like six years ago, I would say yes," Brittany said.

"Not to mention that the two of you fell in love really fast after that," Stephanie added, then turned to Tiffany. "So, yes, it counts."

Brittany sighed, clearly satisfied with the way things worked out. Of course, given the fact that she was married to a wealthy horse rancher who thought the sun rose and shone just for her, and that the two of them were raising his niece as their daughter as well as their three-year-old son, there was no reason for her not to be pleased. Tiffany would be just as content in those circumstances. But her life hadn't worked out that way. She hadn't fallen in love with a man who loved her with his whole heart. A man who would sacrifice everything for the ones he loved. No, she'd fallen for a liar and cheat who would sacrifice anything and anyone to protect his own interests, not caring who he hurt in the process.

"You're right. It didn't take long for our fake relationship to become real. But that's not the point here," Brittany said.

"Then what is the point?" Tiffany asked.

"The point is that you don't need to spend a lot of time with Ellis in order to fall in love with him. If the feelings are real, you won't be able to resist them for long."

"But I don't want to fall in love with Ellis." Tiffany knew she was whining, but she couldn't help it.

"In the words of Mick Jagger, you can't always get what you want," Brittany said.

"But if you're lucky," Stephanie added before singing, "you'll get what you need."

"What I *need* is to stop talking about Ellis," Tiffany said firmly.

No, what she needed was to stop falling for Ellis. But Brittany and Mick were right. She couldn't always get what she wanted.

Chapter Eight

Ellis parked his pickup in the guest spot in the lot for Tiffany's apartment building and blew out a long breath. He'd known that she wouldn't be staying in Bronco for long, but it sucked knowing that there was no possibility that he would run into her in town. Those unexpected meetings had brightened his day. Though he was loathe to admit it to himself, he'd been very disappointed yesterday when she'd told him that she couldn't spend the rest of the day with him. He'd still been floating on air from the night they'd spent in each other's arms and hadn't been ready to return to Earth so soon. Making love to her had been something beyond his previous experiences. She'd touched a place inside him that no other woman had ever approached. In fact, he hadn't even known that place had existed before that night.

In retrospect, it was probably best that he'd had a day away from her. He'd needed the distance so he could regain his equilibrium. The last thing he needed was to get too attached to her. Neither of them was looking for a romantic relationship. Though he was open to changing his mind if circumstances changed, Tiffany had been abundantly clear that she wasn't. He wasn't looking to have his heart broken.

Ellis hopped out of his truck and took the elevator to Tiffany's apartment. When his pulse began to race in anticipation, he took a deep breath and reminded himself that they were only friends. Spending the day with her would be no different than spending it with any of his other female friends.

Determined to play it cool, he rang her doorbell and waited. A few moments later the door swung open and Tiffany was standing there.

"Wow. You look great." The words burst out of him before he could control them. So much for playing it cool.

She smiled. "It's nothing special. Just jeans and Stephanie's boots."

"Then it must be the person wearing them. Who knew that a plain cotton shirt could be so sexy?" He tried to put a playful note into his voice to cover up the desire that suddenly consumed him. The last time he'd been in her apartment, they'd ended up in her bed. He supposed it was too much to hope to cash in his rain check right now. Perhaps he should dare her since that had worked out so well for him before.

Tiffany's smile broadened as she grabbed her purse. "Let's go."

Even though Tiffany told him it wasn't necessary, Ellis insisted on opening the truck door for her and then waited until she fastened her seat belt before taking his place behind the wheel. The conversation flowed nonstop as he drove to his family's ranch. When Ellis exited the highway and turned onto a two-lane road, Tiffany turned to him. "How much farther?"

"Is that the adult version of *are we there yet*?"

Tiffany laughed and something dangerously close to his heart grew warm. He was coming to love that sound just a little too much for his peace of mind.

"I suppose it is. So…"

"Not much longer. About ten minutes or so." He smirked. "That doesn't give you much time to come up with an excuse to avoid riding."

"That's not what I was doing at all."

"Good. Because if you backed out now, I might not be able to handle the disappointment." Though he'd added a bit of humor to his voice, his words held a nugget of truth. He wanted to share an important part of his life with Tiffany. More than that, he wanted her to enjoy today as much as he had enjoyed the concert.

"I'm not backing out. In fact, I think I might have an as-yet undiscovered knack for riding."

"Really? And what gave you that idea?"

"I'm more athletic than I look."

His eyes swept over her body. Before last night, he might not have described her as athletic but now he knew that the word fit. So did sexy. And enthusiastic. Suddenly hot, he rolled down his window, letting in some cool air, then forced those recollections to the recesses of his mind. He tried to pick up the threads of the conversation before it—and he—completely unraveled.

"Well, we'll soon see." He signaled and turned onto a long driveway. "We're here."

He drove past his parents' stately home, staying on

the gravel road until he reached a painted stable. They got out and he let Tiffany look around. Her eyes were filled with surprise. "Wow. This place is gorgeous. It looks like something out of a movie."

Ellis smiled proudly. Despite the struggles of the town, his family ranch was thriving. Six generations of Coreys had worked hard to make it so. If he had his way, the next six generations would be even more successful. "I told you it was beautiful."

"I thought that might have been a bit of pride talking."

"Nah. Just pure honesty. But this is nothing. Wait until we're riding across the range." He let her look around before leading her to the tack room. "We keep the saddles over here."

Tiffany frowned as she looked at the empty stables. "Where are the horses?"

"In the corral. We leave the outside stall doors open so they can come and go as they please. On nice days, they like to run around the corral."

He grabbed blankets and handed them to Tiffany. "You carry these and I'll bring the rest of the tack."

He picked up the saddles, bridles and riding gloves. When they had everything they needed, they went out the back door.

"Wait right here while I get your horse. I thought that you'd feel most comfortable on Daisy."

Ellis hopped over the fence and strode over to a dappled mare who was enjoying the sunshine. Daisy, easily the best natured horse on the ranch, was the one the family chose to let children ride whenever they visited.

She was patient and had a steady gait—the perfect horse for Tiffany's first ride.

Ellis led the mare over to Tiffany. The closer he and Daisy got to Tiffany, the wider her eyes grew and the stiffer her body became. Until this moment, he hadn't understood just how afraid Tiffany was.

"This is Daisy," Ellis said gently, hoping his calm voice would sooth Tiffany's frazzled nerves. "She's the one you'll be riding today."

Tiffany nodded. She was trying to keep up a strong front, but the way she nibbled on her full bottom lip was a sign of her internal struggle. Ellis had grown up around animals, so to him, the horses were trusted friends. But to Tiffany, Daisy must appear to be fifteen hundred pounds of animal waiting to buck her off. Or worse, take a bite out of her.

Tiffany's lips spread into what was a poor facsimile of her normal bright smile. She took a step back and he sighed. She was even more of a city girl than he imagined. She squared her shoulders. "Is it okay to touch her?"

"Of course. You can rub her neck. She likes that."

Tiffany reached out a tentative hand as if she was about to touch fire. When her palm brushed against Daisy, her eyes widened in surprise. "She's so soft. And warm."

"What did you expect?"

"I don't know." Tiffany rubbed her hand over the mare for several minutes, gradually inching closer. The horse never moved. Smiling, Tiffany turned and looked into Ellis's eyes. Hers were now filled with confidence. "I think she will be okay to ride."

"I knew the two of you would get along."

"Which horse are you going to ride?"

"Smokey. He's mine." Ellis gestured to a black stallion who was standing near the fence. His head was raised as if he was waiting to be called over.

Tiffany gasped. "He's huge."

"I know."

"It would probably hurt if you fell off."

"No doubt. That's why I don't fall off."

Ellis expertly saddled and bridled Daisy. Then in one smooth move he swung up into the saddle and looked down at Tiffany. He knew that he was needlessly showing off, but he couldn't help himself. He was going to take any opportunity he had to impress her. He dismounted smoothly. "See how easy that was."

"Sure. Piece of cake." Her voice was dry as a desert. "Move aside and I'll hop right on."

"I'm going to walk you through it step by step. My main purpose was to show you how calm Daisy is. She didn't even blink when I got in the saddle." That was the only reason he was willing to admit to Tiffany.

"Okay. I hope she's as patient with a beginner as she was with a pro. I don't want to make her mad."

"I wouldn't have offered her to you if I thought she would do anything to hurt you," Ellis said quietly.

Tiffany must have heard the sincerity in his voice because her shoulders relaxed. "What should I do?"

"Stand on her left side. Now put your left foot in the stirrup and swing your right leg over her body."

Tiffany nodded, then followed his instructions. Ellis quickly adjusted the stirrups and took a step back. He looked at Tiffany and chuckled. "You're going to have to open your eyes."

"In a second. I just need to get my bearings."

"Take your time. I'll wait here until you feel comfortable."

"Really?" The hope in her voice touched him in a way he hadn't expected. Didn't she know she could rely on him?

"Of course. This is supposed to be fun for you, not some type of challenge. If you don't feel comfortable, we can do something else." But that would only provide evidence in support of her belief that they were very different from each other. He didn't know why it was so important to convince her that she was wrong, but it was. He needed her to see how much they had in common and that a relationship between them wasn't far-fetched.

She opened her eyes and looked at him. "I really want to see your ranch. It's such a big part of your life."

"There are other ways of doing that. We can always take a four-wheeler."

"No," she said, her voice filled with determination. "I'm going to ride this horse. I'm not a mouse. I'm a woman."

"Hear you roar?" he said, chuckling.

"I may not be ready to roar, but I'm not going to whimper either. Is there something in between?"

"I'll have to think about that and get back to you. In

the meantime, I'll get Smokey so we can hit the road. Figuratively, since there is no road."

Once Ellis was seated in Smokey's saddle, he glanced over at Tiffany. She didn't appear to be as scared as she'd been before her great pronouncement. Now she looked perplexed.

"Ready to go?" he asked.

"Uh. I think there's a slight problem."

"What's that?" He gave her a once over. Everything looked okay to him.

"I don't know how to get this thing started. How do I make her go?"

Ellis smothered a smile. "Squeeze your legs gently and lean forward. That's the clue that she needs to get going."

"It would be so much easier if I could just say, 'let's go, horsey' and clap my hands. You know, like with a dog."

"Do you have a dog?"

"Well, no, but my brother has a mastiff. I thought that thing was huge." She shook her head. "Clearly I was wrong. This horse is so much bigger."

"But you can't ride a dog."

"True."

"You'll get used to Daisy's size in no time. Once you relax you're going to have a great time. Before you know it, you'll be begging me to take you riding again."

She gave him a look he couldn't decipher before she gently squeezed her legs, barely moving them. Daisy didn't budge.

"You're going to have to squeeze harder than that."

"I don't want to hurt her."

"You won't."

Tiffany tried again, her motion once more barely perceptible.

Ellis raised his eyebrows and shook his head. "Harder."

"She had better not get mad at me," Tiffany warned. She squeezed her legs harder this time. Daisy took a step forward. And then another. Tiffany looked at him, her eyes wide with panic. "How do you stop this thing?"

"Just gently pull back on the reins."

Tiffany pulled on them as instructed. Daisy stopped immediately. Tiffany blew out her breath and gave a strangled laugh. "I suppose I should have asked that before I got her started."

"I should have told you. But we have it all covered now. So let's give it a go, shall we?"

She nodded and squeezed her knees, giving Daisy the go sign. They started slowly across the grass, riding side by side. Ellis knew that Tiffany was concentrating on riding, so he didn't try to engage her in conversation as they headed toward the trail. Her eyebrows were drawn and she was biting her bottom lip in a way that he found incredibly sexy. Memories of kissing those lips flashed in his mind and he smiled. He sincerely hoped that they would be able to spend another night wrapped in each other's arms. Soon.

After about ten minutes of going so slowly they were practically standing still, Tiffany glanced over at him. "I'm ready to go faster."

"Okay."

Ellis showed Tiffany how to get Daisy to speed up. After a minute, they were going somewhere between a walk and a trot. He noticed with satisfaction that Tiffany was no longer tense and she had lost the air of terror that had been surrounding her. Now she actually seemed to be having a good time.

"Yeehaw!" she exclaimed, a broad grin on her face.

"What?"

"Isn't that what you say when you're going fast on a horse?"

"First, we aren't going fast. Not even close. Second, I have never said 'yeehaw' in my life. In fact, I've never heard anyone say it. Besides you that is."

She grimaced. "Obviously I've been misled by TV shows."

"Yeah. Lucky for you, I'm the only one who heard it."

"I'm trusting your discretion."

"Is that right?" He grinned.

She turned her head and looked at him, a smile playing on her full and extremely kissable lips. "I notice that you didn't say something like 'Of course you can trust me.'"

"Of course you can trust me," he mimicked.

She laughed. "That so lacked sincerity. You were the kid who always got into trouble, weren't you?"

"It depends on how you define trouble."

"I'll take that as a yes. And since I joined my brothers in mischief from time to time, I won't hold it against you."

"Really? Perhaps we can get into trouble together."

"What do you have in mind?"

Making love in the soft grass under the bright sunshine flashed in his mind. His face must have revealed his thoughts, because Tiffany shook her head. “Think of something else, Cowboy.”

He threw his head back and laughed. “I’ll do my best. But after the other night it’s really hard to think of anything else.” That night had been memorable. One for the books. No doubt he would be thinking of that night when he was eighty years old.

She turned and looked directly at him. Her eyes were serious. “Yes. Five stars. Best time I ever had. But don’t go falling in love with me, okay? We’re simply friends who kiss.”

“We did more than kiss,” he pointed out. “Three times.”

“Okay. And more,” she said softly.

He knew the ‘and more’ referred to making love, but a part of him wondered if the ‘and more’ could one day mean more than friends. More than lovers. The notion wasn’t as shocking as it might have been. After all, he liked Tiffany. A lot. If the situation was different, he would have pursued her. And caught her. But the circumstances were the same today as before. He was still trying to figure out his next move. He liked being a rancher, but he felt that there was more he should do with his life. Until he knew for sure what that *more* was, he didn’t want to become romantically involved.

“This is really a lot of fun,” Tiffany said after a while. “I don’t know why I was so scared of horses. Daisy is big but she’s a dream.”

"Most of the time, we discover that our fears aren't as big as we made them out to be."

"True."

"You're welcome to come back and ride any time you like."

"There are lots of ranches much closer to my home. Some of my extended family have horses. I could always join one of them on a ride."

"You could," he said slowly. "But you wouldn't have such stellar company."

She tilted her head in that familiar way that he was coming to love. "Is that right?"

"You know it."

"I suppose you do have a point there." She grinned mischievously. "But I'm sure I could muddle through somehow."

"I wouldn't be much of a gentleman if I forced you to settle for less. No, we'll just have to work it out so you can ride with me any time you choose."

"How very gallant of you."

Ellis was about to reply when he heard the sound of horses hooves. The sound grew louder as they drew nearer to them. He knew who it was without looking. So much for having time alone with Tiffany. "It sounds like we're about to have company." Being invaded was a more accurate way to describe it.

She looked in the direction of the pounding hooves. The riders were close enough for him to make out. "Who are they?"

"My sister and brothers." He managed to keep the irritation from his voice. Barely.

When Tiffany agreed to go riding with him, he'd called Aaron to let him know his plans and asked his brother to cover his ranch duties for him. Ellis had foolishly believed that Aaron would keep the information about the date to himself. He should have known better. But he couldn't fault Aaron entirely. Michelle had probably pounced on him the second Aaron let them know Ellis wouldn't be at work today. She had a knack of knowing whenever any of her brothers had a secret and could worm it out of them, wearing down their resistance.

"Did you set this up?" Tiffany asked, her voice dripping with suspicion. Her lovely eyes were narrowed, proof that she believed he had set out to pressure her to become more than friends who kiss.

"God, no," he said. "The last thing I want is them pestering me."

"Okay. Just checking." She sighed but didn't seem relieved. Her jaw was clenched and her shoulders were stiff. The tension that she had shed was back again. Clearly the idea of meeting his family distressed her. But then, since she'd already made it plain that she didn't want a relationship, he could see how she could think he was doing an end run. Knowing she thought he could be so sneaky hurt, but he shoved the pain aside. He didn't do self-pity. Not only that, her feelings were more important than his.

"Don't worry. They're incredibly annoying, but on the whole they're good people. Which has me wondering why they've decided to descend on us like a pack of locusts."

"You don't think anything is wrong, do you? Like with your parents or grandparents?"

"No. If there was a problem, they wouldn't be together looking for me like an old-fashioned search party. Besides, I have my phone. They would have called. They're just being nosy. I told one of my brothers that we would be riding today. Obviously I confided in the wrong one."

She laughed. "When it comes to doing something with a member of the opposite sex, I don't think there is a right one. At least not in my family."

"I'm glad you understand. Should we try to outrun them?"

She looked at him as if he had lost his mind. "Hello. I'm still the same Tiffany who had never been on a horse before today. No, I think we need to admit defeat."

"*This* time. But if it makes you feel better, I'll pay them all back later."

"When they least expect it?" she said with a grin.

"Oh, no. I want them to expect it. I want them to live in a constant state of dread, looking over their shoulders and wondering when I'm going to strike."

"Wow. That's positively sinister. And I love it. But remind me to never get on your bad side."

"You don't have to worry about that, Tiffany. You'll always be on my good side."

The smile she flashed him made his heart race. Though he'd been flirting, there was something more beneath his words. Something he wasn't ready to deal with head-on.

Luckily, and yet unluckily, his siblings reached them.

"Hi," Michelle said as she looked between Ellis and Tiffany. She was so transparent that Ellis could practically see the wheels turning in her head. Michelle smiled and he wondered just what his sister saw.

"Hello," Tiffany said, smiling in return.

"Aaron said that Ellis was using your presence as a way to get out of work," Michelle continued, her eyes dancing with mischief, "so we decided the least we could do was annoy him for a moment. I hope you don't mind."

Tiffany laughed. "I suppose that's okay. I didn't know that Ellis was doing that."

"I wasn't," he protested. "Michelle's making a joke. A bad one."

"I'm Shane," his brother said. There was an authority in his voice that left no question that he was the oldest sibling.

"It's nice to meet you, Shane."

"This is Tristan and this is Aaron," he said, indicating the two men who rode on either side of him. They each smiled and nodded as he called their names.

"It's nice to meet you both," Tiffany said, smiling at one and then the other.

"Where are you riding to?" Michelle asked as if it were her business.

"I have no idea," Tiffany said. "Where are we going, Ellis?"

He sighed. "I thought we would go out to the old swimming hole."

"Ah. Do you plan on telling Tiffany about the time

Shane dared you to jump from the top of the tree into the water?" Michelle asked.

His siblings looked at each other and laughed.

"That wasn't among my plans," he said, wondering if it would be rude to tell them to go away.

"But now I need to hear the story," Tiffany said, her smile growing.

"It is a good one," Michelle said. "Very funny."

"How would you know?" Ellis asked. "You weren't even there."

"Only because you guys always left me behind while you went on great adventures."

"We were protecting you," Tristan said.

"From what? A good time?"

"Weeks of cleaning out the stalls as punishment," Aaron said.

"Why?" Tiffany asked.

"I kind of fell wrong and ended up with a broken leg," Ellis explained.

"Is there a right way to fall?" Tiffany asked.

"You jumped too soon," Shane said. "You were supposed to go to the end of the branch and then jump. I still don't think I should have been punished because you went before you were over the water."

"What about me and Tristan?" Aaron asked. "We were only witnesses."

"Innocent bystanders," Tristan added.

"Bystanders who goaded me on," Ellis added.

"Don't tell me. Another double-dog dare," Tiffany guessed. She rolled her eyes.

He nodded.

"Is there any part of your body that hasn't been sacrificed on the altar of the male ego?" Tiffany asked.

"Wait a minute," Shane said as Aaron and Tristan sputtered. "There are some things a man has to do. He can't walk away from a double-dog dare. Not if he has any self-respect."

Michelle looked at Tiffany. "You know, if you're really quiet when they turn their heads, you can hear the rocks rolling around in there."

Tiffany laughed. "Have you tried talking sense into them?"

"For years. It doesn't work."

Tiffany shared Michelle's smile and nodded. Though it didn't make a difference in the long run, Ellis was glad to see that Tiffany got along well with his siblings.

They talked and joked around for a few more minutes until Shane spoke. "We rode out here so we could meet you, Tiffany, and say hello. Unlike our brother, we need to get back to work."

Ellis's brothers and sister said their goodbyes, then turned and rode away.

"They're nice," Tiffany said once she and Ellis were alone.

"I suppose they're tolerable in small doses."

"It's obvious that you're all very close."

He nodded. "I got lucky in the sibling department."

"You and your brothers look a lot alike."

"Sort of. But I think you'll agree that I'm the most handsome of the bunch."

Tiffany laughed. "If not the most modest."

He grinned. "I had to leave some good traits for the rest of them. It's only fair."

"You are too much," Tiffany said. She looked around. "How far are we from the swimming hole?"

"Not far. Why? Are you thinking of daring me to do something?"

"No. And definitely not the dare you're hoping for."

"A man can always dream," Ellis said, wiggling his eyebrows suggestively as they set off again.

When they reached the swimming hole twenty minutes later, Ellis helped Tiffany dismount, holding her by the waist until she was standing on solid ground. He released her and she wobbled a little. Reaching out, Tiffany grabbed the front of his shirt and looked up at him. "I can't believe I forgot how to walk."

"You're not used to riding horses. Take a minute and the Jell-O sensation will go away."

In less than a minute, Tiffany had regained her balance and stepped away. He sighed. Holding her against his body had felt good.

"So, which tree did you jump from?" Tiffany asked as she walked around. His eyes were drawn to the gentle sway of her curvy bottom and he took two longs strides to catch up to her. The breeze blew a lock of her hair into her face and she swept it away before he could.

He pointed to a tall, sturdy oak, not far from the water's edge.

"Oh, you must have been out of your mind," she said, looking up.

"It wasn't quite so tall back then. And I didn't climb all the way to the top."

"If I was your mother, cleaning the stables for a few weeks would have been the least of your punishment."

"I didn't have to do that," he told her. "Remember, my leg was broken."

"So you got away with it?"

"Not even close. I had to write a five-hundred word paper on the stupidity—my mother's exact word—of doing something dangerous simply because of a dare."

"Given the fact that you are still giving in to dares, I don't think you learned your lesson."

He shrugged. "I'm a work in progress."

Ellis and Tiffany walked around the edge of the water until they came upon a large boulder. Tiffany sat down and scooted over, making a space for him beside her. He sat down and her sweet scent wafted around him. A bird's song filled the air and Ellis was filled with a feeling of contentment. He could sit here forever with Tiffany and not need another thing to be happy. She leaned her head against his shoulder and sighed.

After a while, the feeling of peace was replaced with desire. Being this close to her awakened a strong yearning in him. Ignoring the myriad reasons why he shouldn't, Ellis lifted Tiffany's chin and stared into her eyes. Her eyes reflected the lust that was steadily building inside him. As if pulled by an unseen force, he leaned down and kissed her lips. They were soft and warm. Receptive. In an instant, the kiss went from searching to scorching. As their tongues tangled, Ellis began to burn. The kiss only lasted a few minutes, but he knew that he had to end it before things got out of hand.

He'd been teasing when he'd talked about the two

of them getting into trouble out here. Not only was the weather too cool to take off their clothes, despite the heat they were generating, his siblings knew where he was. He didn't want one of them to decide to annoy him again and catch him and Tiffany at an inopportune moment. Just the thought was like a bucket of cold water being poured on his head and he pulled away.

"What happened?" Tiffany asked, clearly confused by the abrupt way he'd ended things. She looked at him, her eyes hazy with desire.

He shook his head. "My brothers and sister."

"Enough said." She looked around as if she expected them to pop out from behind one of the trees. "I suppose you must have done something like that in your past. Now you're the one living in fear of payback."

"I neither confirm nor deny that statement," he said, getting to his feet and then taking her hand and helping her to stand.

"Your non-denial is an admission."

"In my defense, I didn't know anyone was out here. And I certainly had no idea what they were doing. Believe me, when I found out, I immediately ran away, scarred for life. There are some things a man can't unsee no matter how hard he tries. And believe me, I tried. But can I help it if my horse chose that very minute to neigh loudly before I could make a clean getaway?"

Tiffany giggled. "You are a complete mess. No wonder your brothers and sister rode out to bother us. I just hope they remember that I'm an innocent party."

"They will. They liked you."

"I liked them, too."

When they reached the horses, Tiffany grabbed Daisy's reins and then looked at Ellis. "I can do this on my own."

"I know. You're a natural. Just like you said."

"But just in case, be ready to catch me if Daisy doesn't agree."

He nodded. "You can count on me."

After Tiffany was seated in the saddle, Ellis mounted Smokey and they started for the house. As they rode, that feeling of rightness returned. No matter how hard he tried to get rid of it, he couldn't.

And that meant one thing. *Trouble.*

Chapter Nine

The stables were growing larger as Tiffany and Ellis grew nearer and Tiffany blew out a breath. The horseback ride was coming to an end. Today had been as far away from her normal activities as anything she had ever done, but she was happy that she'd taken a chance and stepped outside of her comfort zone. Though initially she'd had mixed feelings about the ride, she'd had a wonderful time with Ellis. She wasn't ready to say goodbye to him. But in a few minutes they would be dismounting and there was nothing she could do to change that.

"We didn't go fast or far, but we still need to groom the horses," Ellis said as he led the way into the stable.

"I don't know what you mean, but count me in," Tiffany said, glad to have more time with Ellis. Despite trying to resist, she was becoming attached to him. She'd worry about that later. Now she was going to enjoy the moment. "Just tell me what you want me to do and I'll do it."

"Is that right?" He gave her a devilish grin that set butterflies free in her stomach. She loved the way he flirted with her.

She poked him in the shoulder. His muscle was impressively hard. "Within reason, Cowboy."

"Grooming is basically combing and brushing the horses and checking their hooves for any dirt, rocks or debris they might have picked up on the ride."

"I'm all for brushing Daisy, but I'm not messing with her feet. Just in case she's in a kicking mood."

Ellis laughed. "Agreed. I'll do that part."

Ellis gathered the tools. After he'd picked Daisy's hooves, he gave Tiffany a currycomb. As they worked together, a feeling of contentment swept over her. There was something soothing about brushing Daisy. The rhythmic motion was hypnotic. Or perhaps it was Ellis's nearness that was casting a spell on her.

When they were finished, Ellis inspected the mare, then smiled at Tiffany. "I don't think Daisy has been this well groomed in her entire life. You've definitely spoiled her. Now you won't have a choice but to come back again. It's only fair."

Tiffany laughed. "If you say so."

"I do."

They led the horses to their stalls, then Tiffany followed Ellis back outside, her eyes focused on his broad shoulders. She couldn't help admiring the way they tapered down to his trim waist, how—

He stopped so abruptly that Tiffany bumped into him.

"Oh, no," he said.

"What's wrong?" she asked, looking around. Everything seemed okay to her. Not that she would know since this was her first time visiting the ranch.

"My parents are sitting on their patio. I bet they know

that you met my sister and brothers. There are no secrets in this family. No doubt they want to meet you, too." He gave her a rueful look. "Sorry about this. I suppose we can wave and keep going to the truck."

The thought of making a run for it was so ludicrous that Tiffany couldn't help laughing. "We don't need to do anything that extreme. I think I can survive talking to your parents for a few minutes."

"Are you sure? Because I don't want you to think that I set you up."

"I don't. I was wrong to accuse you that way before. I think a part of me knew you wouldn't do that to me. Besides, Michelle and your brothers were great." She smirked. "And you have one or two good qualities yourself."

He laughed. "Don't go overboard with the compliments. It might go to my head."

"I just meant that all of you Corey kids are a reflection of your parents, so I'm sure they will be great, too."

"Come on. I'll introduce you."

As they walked toward the older couple, Tiffany managed to maintain a cool exterior. Despite the calm smile on her face, she was a tiny bit nervous about meeting Ellis's parents. The tension was as unexpected as it was ridiculous. Even though she hoped that they would like her—nobody wanted to be disliked—their feelings about her really were immaterial. It wasn't as if she was about to be their daughter-in-law and needed their approval or acceptance. She probably wouldn't even see them again after today.

The couple stood up as Ellis and Tiffany walked over.

They smiled warmly and the knot of apprehension in Tiffany's stomach disappeared.

Ellis kissed his mother's cheek and then made the introductions. "Mom, Dad, this is my friend Tiffany Brandt. Tiffany, these are my parents, Patty and Joseph Corey."

Tiffany smiled, holding out her hand. "It's nice to meet you, Mr. and Mrs. Corey."

"It's lovely meeting you," his mother said, taking Tiffany's hand. "And please, call us Patty and Joseph."

"Take a load off," Joseph said, pulling out a chair from beneath the table beside the firepit. His smile held a hint of mischief, leaving Tiffany no doubt where Ellis had gotten that part of his personality.

"Thank you," Tiffany said, sitting.

"We can't stay long," Ellis said, settling into the chair beside her.

"Surely you can stay long enough for a quick snack. I just iced this," Patty said, gesturing to the cake on the table, "and the coffee is fresh." Her voice held a hint of disappointment that touched Tiffany's heart.

"I wouldn't say no to a piece of cake and a mug of coffee," Tiffany said. She appreciated that Ellis was trying to keep her from feeling uncomfortable, but she'd been raised to be considerate. She couldn't throw his parents' hospitality back into their faces. Not when they were trying so hard to put her at ease.

"Wonderful." Patty cut and plated generous slices of cake while Joseph poured the coffee and distributed silverware. The two worked as a team, as if they had done this hundreds of times over the years.

"How did you enjoy your ride?" Joseph asked, taking a bite of cake.

"I had a great time," Tiffany said. "Daisy is a sweet horse. I didn't get to see a lot of your ranch, but what I did see of it is quite beautiful."

"Thank you," Joseph replied, the pride in his voice reflected in his eyes.

"What part did you show her?" Patty asked.

"We rode around the east acreage and ended up by the old swimming hole," Ellis said.

"Did he tell you about that foolishness?" Patty asked, shaking her head. "Jumping out of a tree like he didn't have a lick of sense and nearly breaking his neck."

"I was twelve," Ellis said.

"And don't forget that his brother dared him," Joseph added as if that explained it all.

"Double-dog dared," Ellis clarified.

"As if that made a difference," Patty said.

"It does," Joseph and Ellis said in unison. They grinned at each other in complete understanding.

"Do you see what I have to deal with?" Patty asked, turning to look at Tiffany as she feigned exasperation. Her eyes sparkled with affection as she glanced between her husband and her son. "It's a wonder that Ellis made it to adulthood in one piece."

"Oh, the stories we could tell you," Joseph added. He'd gone from being Ellis's ally and was now on his wife's side.

"Another time," Ellis said, coming to his feet. "Between you and the rest of this family, you're going to convince Tiffany that I don't have a sense of self-preservation."

"Or any sense at all," Patty said, laughing. "But we love you anyway."

"It was nice meeting you," Tiffany said as she and Ellis's parents rose.

"Same here. Please feel free to come back anytime," Patty said. "If you're free for Easter, we'd love to have you for dinner."

Tiffany was surprised and pleased by the unexpected invitation. "Thank you. I'm not sure of my plans, but I'll let Ellis know so he can get back to you one way or the other."

"Good enough," Joseph said.

As Tiffany walked beside Ellis to his truck, she felt a sense of rightness. A feeling of belonging that she didn't quite understand. Nor did she want to interrogate it. She paused and took one last glance around the ranch. It was positively beautiful. From the stately house to the well-kept buildings and the acres and acres of land, everything was perfection.

"You don't have to soak it all in as if you're trying to seal the memory in your mind," Ellis said as if he knew what she'd been doing. "You have an open invitation, remember?"

"I know. I just want to preserve the image until next time."

Ellis opened the truck door for her. Once he was sitting behind the wheel, he glanced over at her, his expression serious. "Here's hoping that *next time* comes soon."

"We'll see," Tiffany said, deliberately noncommittal. She shifted in her seat, then said, "Your parents are great."

"I know. I wouldn't trade them for the world." Ellis grinned. "But I have no doubt there were times they would have traded me for a pack of chewing gum if they could have gotten anyone to take them up on the offer."

Tiffany laughed. "It does sound like you were a bit of a challenging child."

"You don't know the half of it. But despite some bumps, bruises and a few broken bones, I turned out okay. I'm no longer *challenging* as you called me. Now I'm a son they can be proud of."

"I got the impression that they were always proud of you." She smiled. "And exhausted by you."

"My mother used to tell me that she hoped that I would have a child just like me."

"Oh. Mothers love to hex their kids like that. It's written in the mother's handbook."

"Did your mother say that, too?"

Tiffany nodded. "Of course. But in my case it was more of a blessing than a curse. I was the perfect child, you see."

Ellis laughed so hard that Tiffany thought he might stop breathing. When he'd regained control of himself, he glanced at her. There were tiny tears in his eyes. "I knew you had a good sense of humor, but you're funnier than I thought. You're hilarious."

Tiffany tried to keep a stern expression on her face, but before long she was laughing with him. She, too, had been a challenging child.

•

"A good sense of humor is important to making any relationship work," Ellis said abruptly.

"We're just friends," Tiffany reminded him.

"Friends who kiss," Ellis said with a wink.

"As long as we understand each other." She was becoming so comfortable with Ellis that she also needed this reminder.

"We do." He was silent for a while. When he spoke again, his voice was casual. Perhaps too casual. "So, what do you think about marriage?"

Where did that come from? They'd just said they were only friends, so why was he asking for her opinion on marriage? "What kind of question is that?"

"A simple one." He shrugged, trying to act as if this wasn't a big deal. "My parents have been married for close to forty years. I know your parents have been married for as long—if not longer. So we've both gotten an up close and personal view of happy marriages."

"That's true. I suppose marriage can be great and a source of happiness. For *some* people." She just didn't think she was one of them. Not after the way things had ended with the snake she'd planned to spend the rest of her life with. There was something about being so completely betrayed that removed the hope and romance from a woman's heart. After that experience, it was hard to want to take a chance again.

"Take a breath. I'm not proposing to you, so there's no need for you to panic. We're still getting to know each other. Either of us might discover something that is a deal-breaker."

Tiffany took a breath, but it didn't make her feel any

less tense. Why was Ellis talking about deal-breakers? There was no deal to break. They weren't going to have a serious relationship. This was a fling.

"But right now?" Ellis continued, "I believe there is something special growing between us. Something I haven't felt before and can't put a name to. But I want to pursue it. Who knows? Over time I think it could become real. I think the feeling could deepen." He inhaled and blew out the breath. Then he glanced at her and she read the sincerity in his eyes. And it scared her half to death. "I just want to let you know that I'm not feeling casual anymore."

"Oh." She managed to force the word out of her suddenly dry mouth.

"That's all you have to say?"

"You've caught me off guard here, so I'm going to need a minute."

"Sorry. You're right. Take all the time you need to gather your thoughts."

There wasn't enough time in the world for that. Her thoughts had scattered all over the universe and bringing them back together into a coherent statement would be hard if not impossible. But she couldn't tell him that. He might press her for a reason and she might blurt out everything—telling him how she'd been duped by her ex. She could only imagine how his image of her would change if he knew that story. Right now, he thought she was smart. Funny. *Magnificent.* She didn't want to reveal how stupid she'd been. She didn't want to lower his opinion of her. It was bad enough that her family and close friends knew the truth. At least the broad strokes. The most humiliating details would go to the grave with her. But Ellis didn't need to know any of it.

"I really like you, Ellis," she finally said when the silence dragged way past what was comfortable for her. "I think you already know that."

"I feel like there's a 'but' on the way."

Tiffany sighed. "We're just so different. You know, I have city sensibilities and you live on a ranch. A beautiful ranch, but a ranch nonetheless. It's in the middle of..." *Nowhere...* "the country."

"It's not as if we're forbidden to leave. It's not a prison. We can and actually do go to town quite often."

Tenacity. That place was so far from what she was used to that it would be laughable if the whole situation wasn't so sad. She didn't want to hurt Ellis's feelings, but she had to make him see reason. "Yes. But it's not as if you can get a smoothie whenever the urge hits you. At home, I can be at Bronco Java and Juice in twenty minutes from just about any place in town. It would take many more times than that from your ranch. Or even from Tenacity."

"I hear what you're saying. But geography doesn't have to be an insurmountable problem. Look at Shane and Remi. Shane lives on the ranch and Remi travels all over the country with the rodeo. But they're making it work."

"I'm happy things are working out for them. But you and I are not Shane and Remi. We're two different people. We have different interests and lifestyles."

"Our differences don't necessarily mean that we can't be happy together. I can enjoy myself at concerts.

And I like the idea of being able to go to restaurants at night. Getting a smoothie in twenty minutes would be great. And I actually think a visit to the Big Apple would be fun."

Tiffany tried to picture Ellis in Times Square, walking around in his faded jeans, cowboy boots and Stetson. The image was unexpectedly realistic. He had that swagger and confidence that would allow him to be comfortable anyplace. "You can't help but have a good time in New York."

"And you had a good time riding Daisy today. Unless you were only pretending to enjoy yourself."

"You know I had fun," Tiffany said. "Riding Daisy and seeing your ranch was great."

"It will only get better the more you ride and the more skilled you become. Nothing is more exhilarating than racing across the ranch on a horse running as fast as it can. Going for a slow ride on a sunny afternoon, then having a relaxing lunch at the watering hole can't be beat."

The pictures he painted were appealing and she could actually imagine herself doing those things and loving every minute. What she couldn't picture herself enjoying was the rest of the time. Life was more than horseback rides and alfresco lunches. Just as she knew it was more than spa days and date nights at fancy restaurants. Those were the highlights in otherwise ordinary days. More than that, she had to make a living. Just where did her florist shop exist in the world he was describing? Certainly not in Tenacity. The town could barely sustain the businesses it had. And the people were struggling to pay for necessities. Extras like flowers? No way they had the money for that.

More importantly, she had worked hard to make her shop in Bronco a success. She'd spent countless long days and nights cultivating a clientele and researching to see what it was that her customers wanted. The goodwill that she had built couldn't be picked up and transported to Tenacity. "Why do things have to change between us? You yourself said that things are fine now. Can't we just keep going along as we are?"

Ellis heard the strain in Tiffany's voice and forced himself to back down. There was so much more that he wanted to say but he didn't want to stress her out. He knew that no amount of argument would convince her to be with him. Either she wanted to be in a relationship with him or she didn't. From her reaction, the answer was obvious. She just wasn't that into him. But that was his problem. He wasn't going to make it hers.

He forced himself to smile. "Sure. We can keep on as friends."

"Friends who kiss," she said with obviously forced levity.

"Friends who kiss," he repeated. His levity was just as forced as hers had been. The ease that they normally shared was nowhere to be found. Things were tense between them now and he had no one to blame but himself. Ellis wanted to kick himself. He should have kept his feelings to himself for a while longer. After all, he and Tiffany hadn't spent much time together. They were still learning about each other. Maybe Tiffany would have come to feel the same way about him if he'd given her more time. *Maybe.* But there was no way of putting the toothpaste back into the tube. He'd said what he'd said. And so had she. Now they had to live with it.

Though he didn't like the end result, he knew it was best that he'd revealed his feelings now instead of keeping quiet. If he hadn't, his feelings for Tiffany would continue to grow unchecked. He would have assumed hers were growing, too. When Tiffany finally got around to telling him the truth, that her feelings hadn't changed, he would have been even more disappointed. It was hard, but he had to face the truth head-on. Tiffany only wanted a casual relationship. A temporary relationship. At least with him. He might not think their differences were too big to overcome, but she did. And that was all that mattered.

It might hurt now, but it was better to face the truth than to live in a fantasy world.

Conversation slowed, then sputtered to a halt. Ellis tried to think of something to say to fill the uncomfortable silence, but nothing came to mind. He was filled with too much disappointment to think of a lighthearted topic that would get them back where they'd been a short time ago.

Tiffany, who had been bursting with conversation before, also seemed unable to come up with anything either. She seemed to want to be anywhere but here. When the silence became too thick, he turned on the radio. They listened to the music for the rest of the drive.

"We're here," he said unnecessarily as he pulled into the guest parking spot.

"You don't have to walk me to my door," Tiffany said before she hopped from his truck.

"Of course I do." He may be disappointed with how things turned out, but she was still his date. And he always escorted his date to her door and saw her safely inside.

When they reached her front door, Tiffany smiled and touched his hand, giving it a gentle squeeze before releasing it. "I really did have a good time today, Ellis. Thank you for inviting me."

"I'm glad to hear it."

They stood looking at each other for a moment, neither of them completely at ease. Tiffany nibbled on her bottom lip and Ellis tapped his thigh. Was it really only a few nights ago that they'd stood in this exact place before going inside and making love until they were both exhausted? That night may as well have happened between two different people. The man and woman who couldn't keep their hands off each other had been replaced by two awkward people who couldn't figure out how to say goodbye. No, Ellis knew how to say goodbye. He leaned over and brushed a gentle kiss against her lips before pulling away. She opened her door and stepped inside, closing it firmly behind her.

Sighing, he walked away. Though he hated to admit it, this was probably the last time that they would see each other.

Chapter Ten

Tiffany checked the screen of her cell phone, although she knew that she hadn't missed a call or a text. Her phone had been tethered to her side from the moment she'd woken up today. The same as it had been every other day since she had gone riding with Ellis. She would have heard him call, but he hadn't.

She walked through her shop again, alternately standing on her tiptoes and squatting, inspecting every inch of the renovations. As expected, the crew had done a wonderful job updating her storefront building. The new refrigerated glass cabinets and open white shelves looked better than she had imagined they would. The flowers had been delivered two hours ago and now the space smelled wonderful.

Tiffany had always felt completely at home here. She'd opened the business with a cash loan from her parents and she'd worked hard to pay back every cent. Her pride in accomplishing that feat was only second to theirs. Now though, as she rearranged the decorative ribbons on the glass counter, she felt a twinge of unease. There was no mistaking where it originated. It came from knowing that things were unsettled with

Ellis. Or worse, the knowledge that their relationship was well and truly over.

Three days had passed since their last date. Three long, lonely days and nights where she hadn't heard a word from him. At first she told herself that he was busy. After all, he'd taken a day off work to go riding with her. It wouldn't be unreasonable for him to put in more time the next day. Maybe even the day after. But she couldn't imagine that he would be so busy that he couldn't find a minute to call her. It only took a few seconds to shoot off a text letting her know that he was thinking of her. But he hadn't. Perhaps because she hadn't crossed his mind.

Over the past three days, Tiffany had thought about reaching out, but she hadn't. She'd made a fool of herself over a man once. She had no intention of doing it a second time and expecting a better result. Besides, it was time to face reality. Ellis wasn't interested in continuing their fling. There was no other explanation.

Tiffany thought about the way he'd kissed her goodbye that last time. The kiss had been lacking the heat and passion of the others they'd shared. This one had been tender. Gentle. Almost wistful. As if he'd been saying a final goodbye. Apparently if he couldn't have a permanent relationship, then he didn't want any relationship at all. Tiffany didn't like it, and she certainly didn't share that view, but it was his prerogative. She just wished he hadn't changed the rules in the middle of the game. If she would have known he would act this way, she would have saved her time and spared her feelings. Because loathe as she was to admit it, she did have feelings for Ellis.

And they were hurting.

The bell over the door jangled and Tiffany looked up, grateful for the interruption. She didn't want to spend more time swimming in a pool of self-pity. The relationship was over and it was time to get on with things. Tiffany pasted on a smile. "Hey, Remi. You're right on time."

"Wow. It looks so good in here," Remi said as she looked around.

Tiffany smiled. "Isn't it gorgeous? I'm so pleased with the way everything turned out. I've been walking around touching things all morning."

"I don't blame you. It's perfect." Remi stepped in front of a refrigerated glass case filled with vases of pink roses. "These are beautiful."

"They are," Tiffany said, coming to stand beside Remi. "Are you thinking of pink roses for your wedding?"

"I don't know what I want." Remi sighed. "We've only just set the date and haven't done any other planning yet. I hope I'm not wasting your time."

"You aren't. You're not the first bride I've consulted with who didn't have all of the details firmed up. But it's never too early to think about flowers. There are so many to choose from that it helps to narrow things down ahead of time. You can look around and discover what you like and what you don't. And starting early gives you plenty of leeway to change your mind."

Remi laughed. "I usually know exactly what I want,

but planning the wedding has turned me into an indecisive person I barely recognize. I want everything to be perfect. I've spent hours online looking at bridal dresses. Right now I have about nine favorites. And the list keeps growing and changing."

"That would be a problem. But have you noticed a pattern? Do the ones you like have similar styles? Puffy sleeves? Lots of sparkles? Straight skirt? Long train?"

Remi frowned. "No such luck. That would make the decision that much easier."

"Well, there's only one thing you can do."

"And that is?"

"Walk down the aisle in one gown. Then while the soloist is singing, duck behind the altar and change into another to say your vows in. I don't know how long your reception is going to be, but I can imagine at least two dress changes there. Possibly three if you work at it," Tiffany said, managing to keep a straight face.

Remi gave Tiffany a confused look before she began to laugh. "I would get behind that plan, but the dresses I like are really expensive and I'm on a budget. I'm going to have to choose one and stick with it."

Tiffany grinned. "Well, there's always the rock-paper-scissors route. Many a decision has been made that way."

Remi laughed again. "You're no more help than my sisters and cousins."

"Sorry," Tiffany said with a laugh. She gave Remi's hand a comforting squeeze and grew serious. "I know that whichever dress you choose, you are going to make a beautiful bride. Shane won't be able to keep his eyes off you."

"Thank you. But enough about my dress drama. Let's talk about flowers."

"I think we're going to have to step back into dress drama for just a minute. Not the bridal dress," Tiffany hastened to add. "Bridesmaid dresses. Have you chosen a color for those yet? Or even a color scheme for the wedding?"

"Not yet."

"Okay. Then we won't worry about colors today. Let's just look at the flowers and go from there. Point out any color and shape you like. I'll see if a pattern develops."

"Are they for the bouquets, church arrangements or centerpieces?"

"Yes. One, two or all of them. Right now just let me know what you like. We can start with what I have in the store and then look through the catalogues."

Remi walked around the shop, pointing out flowers while Tiffany took notes. Remi had eclectic tastes to say the least. She liked wildflowers as well as cultured blooms. Bold colors appealed to her as well as whites and ivories. It would be challenging to come up with arrangements that incorporated all of Remi's choices. But Tiffany liked a challenge and she looked forward to coming up with the perfect arrangements.

When Tiffany had shown Remi everything she had in the store, she grabbed several catalogues from a shelf behind the counter.

"Would you like some coffee?" Tiffany asked as she put the catalogues on a round table.

"I would love some."

Tiffany quickly poured two cups in the cozy employee area behind the store, and then she and Remi sat down at the consultation table out front.

Remi added sugar and cream and then took a sip. "So, I hear that you and I might be sisters-in-law one day."

Tiffany sputtered and nearly choked on her coffee. "Where did you hear that?"

Remi gave her a long look. "I was just kidding."

"Oh. Okay." She should have known Remi wasn't serious. Especially since Ellis had ghosted her. Or had they ghosted each other?

"The other day, Shane mentioned that you and Ellis have been spending a lot of time together. He also said that he thought things were getting serious between the two of you."

"Why did he say that?" Tiffany kept her voice neutral. Had Ellis led him to believe that? Or had there been something in the way that Tiffany and Ellis had interacted that gave him that impression?

Remi shrugged. "If I had to guess, it's because Ellis doesn't usually bring women to the ranch. I've gotten to know Ellis a bit since Shane and I started dating. Though he's playful, there is a serious side to him. He's a good man."

"A good man who lives in Tenacity." That wasn't the only reason Tiffany had kept Ellis at a distance, or even the biggest one. But it was a problem that they would have had to face sooner or later if they'd wanted a serious relationship and not just a fling. Not that she did.

"I know. And I can imagine what you're thinking. Tenacity isn't at all like Bronco. There aren't the restaurants and boutiques that you're used to. But when you look beneath the surface, you'll notice the similarities. The people in Tenacity are kind and considerate and believe in family—just like here."

"I know," Tiffany admitted. "I liked the people that I met. Including Shane."

"He is great," Remi said, a dreamy smile on her face. "And believe me, I didn't think I would be able to adjust to life in Tenacity. But for different reasons than yours. I'm third-generation rodeo, so I've spent most of my life on the road."

"You and your sisters made a home in Bronco."

"True. But that wasn't the original plan. We'd only intended to stay in town for a few months. Then one by one my sisters fell in love with local men and built lives in Bronco. Then my cousins came to town and they met men and got married, too. I suppose it's my turn to settle down. I'll just be living in Tenacity, which isn't very far away in the grand scheme of things."

"It is if you have to commute every day which I would have to do in order to get here to my shop. I've spent a lot of time making my business a success. I can't just walk away from it just because I met a nice man. Starting over would he hard and the likelihood of a florist thriving in Tenacity is low."

"I get that. And it would require some compromise

on both of your parts. But that's not the real issue, is it?" Remi continued slowly. Insightfully.

Under other circumstances, Tiffany would have given a nonanswer. Remi was a customer after all, and Tiffany preferred to keep things strictly business when she was at work. But she liked Remi. They were sort of family. Besides, the conversation had already veered into personal territory. Not to mention that Remi already knew about Tiffany and Ellis's relationship. "Not entirely."

"If you want to tell me to mind my business, feel free to do so. I won't be offended. But I am a good listener. And I know how to keep a secret. Nothing you tell me will go any further."

"You won't even tell Shane?"

"Nope. My lips are sealed." Remi pantomimed zipping her lips and throwing the key over her shoulder.

What could it hurt? Tiffany took a breath. "Well, I do like Ellis. A lot. We agreed that things between us would be casual. Temporary. And we were having a great time together."

"Until?" Remi prodded gently.

"Until he decided to change the rules and make our relationship serious. Take a chance and see where things went." Tiffany ran a finger over the rim of her cup. "A part of me wanted to take the risk, but I'm scared. I've been hurt before and it's not an experience I'm anxious to repeat. And Ellis and I are so different. I can't see how things would ever work. In the end, one or both of us would be hurt. It's inevitable."

"Are you hurting now?"

Tiffany nodded. "I haven't talked to Ellis in three days. I didn't expect to miss him this much—we were only friends for a short time—but I do." She swallowed painfully. "My heart longs to see him. I miss laughing and talking with him. But I just can't take that risk."

"Does Ellis know what happened in the past?"

"No. I was such a fool." Tiffany shook her head. Even now, years later, her face burned in remembered embarrassment. She hated to think of how naive she'd been. How trusting. How *stupid.*

"It happens to the best of us," Remi said. "But those bad experiences teach us to be better judges of character. Now you're able to tell a good man from a jerk. You already know that a good man is hard to find. And a good man who's willing to put his heart on the line? That's even rarer. I think you should tell Ellis the truth. Tell him why you're scared. Unless you really want to walk away."

The idea of not being with Ellis ever again was too painful to think about. But she wasn't sure she was ready to take the risk. Not when he'd walked away from her so easily.

The bell over the door jingled, putting an end to their conversation. But then, there really wasn't that much more to say.

A well-dressed man stalked into the store and looked around. Then he sniffed and frowned as if he'd smelled something unpleasant. Though he hadn't said a word, his manner rubbed Tiffany the wrong way. But he was a customer.

"Welcome to Tiffany in Bloom. I'm Tiffany. How can I help you?"

"I'm Brad Bruckner," he said, as if the name was supposed to mean something to her. His voice was a shade too loud and filled with self-importance. "I want some flowers. Obviously."

Tiffany pasted on a smile. Dealing with the public meant putting up with all kinds of behavior from customers that she would never tolerate in her personal life. "Well, you came to the right place." *Obviously.* "Would you like a bouquet of mixed flowers or one type of flower in particular?"

He waved a hand as if such questions were a waste of his precious time. "I want the most expensive flowers that you have. And put them in the biggest, most expensive vase in the store. They're a gift for a woman."

"Oh. Well, to be honest, in my experience, women don't necessarily like a flower because of the cost. One woman might prefer a bunch of daisies while another might like lilacs or roses. Or they might like one particular color or scent. If you tell me what your woman friend likes I can come up with something she is sure to love."

He laughed scornfully. "That's a total load of crap."

"Excuse me?" Tiffany raised an eyebrow, somehow managing to maintain a professional tone. It would be so satisfying to throw him out, but she wouldn't. Not yet. If she threw out every customer who had bad manners, she wouldn't be in business for long.

"I can tell that you believe what you're spouting, but let me set you straight. Women care about one thing and one thing only. And that's money. *M-O-N-E-Y.* Period. She'll like the flowers once she learns that they were the most expensive ones in the shop."

Tiffany bit her tongue. She'd never seen this man before and if she was really lucky, he would never darken her door again. "If that's what you want."

"It is. And let me tell you something else. I'm about to come into a lot of money. More money than you can dream of making with this little store. And when I do, I'll be able to get any woman I want." The way he leered at Tiffany made her feel in desperate need of a shower. She didn't care how much money he was coming into. He would never be able to get her. "Or any *women* that I want."

Tiffany grabbed an exquisite crystal vase.

"Do you have a bigger one that that? I want a whole bunch of flowers. And remember, money is no object. I want the one that costs the most." He pulled out a wad of cash and waved it under her nose to prove his point.

Tiffany didn't bother to tell him that the vase she'd chosen *was* the most expensive. Instead, she put it back on the shelf, then picked up the biggest vase in the store.

"That's what I'm talking about. Now fill it to the brim with flowers. And don't use all that cheap white stuff you florists use to take up the space."

"Baby's breath."

"Whatever it's called. I don't want it so don't stick it in there. I'm paying for flowers and only flowers."

"Got it." Tiffany prided herself on her ability to get along with even the most unpleasant customers, but this odious guy was stretching the limits of her patience.

Despite her annoyance, she was determined to make a beautiful bouquet for the unlucky recipient. Working as fast as she could while doing a job worthy of her name, she constructed the biggest arrangement the vase could hold. She left it on the counter while she tallied up the cost. The man didn't bat an eye when he saw the total. Instead he placed several large bills into her hand. She headed to the cash register. "Let me get your change."

Brad Bruckner shook his head and picked up the vase. "Keep it. There's going to be a lot more of that coming my way."

Tiffany watched as the horrible man walked through her shop, knocking over a bucket of daisies as he went. She didn't move until she heard the door close behind him. Then she picked up the bucket he'd carelessly knocked over, grabbed a paper towel and wiped up the water that had spilled from the container. When everything was returned to order, she went back over to Remi who'd watched the entire conversation with a look of horror on her face.

"Wow," Remi said. "What a piece of work."

"That about sums it up." Tiffany shook her head. "I don't know which woman he thinks he'll be able to win over with that attitude of his."

"Women," Remi said. "Plural."

Tiffany wrinkled her nose. "I can't see one—much less more than one—woman being that desperate, no matter how much money is coming his way."

"Do you think he's about to knock off some unsuspecting rich relative?"

"Way to let your imagination get the best of you."

Tiffany giggled. "He probably has a pocket full of lottery tickets."

Remi laughed, then gave Tiffany a wry look. "But the sad thing is there are more Brad Bruckners in the world than there are Ellis Coreys. If you like Ellis, let him know. Before it's too late."

Tiffany nodded. She'd been a fool before. Or had she been fooled? She needed to think about that a little more. But did it matter now? She wasn't sure that Ellis was still interested in her. After all, he hadn't reached out to her. Perhaps after having more time to think about it, he'd realized that she was right. They were too different for a relationship to last. She needed to accept that and leave their relationship in the past.

"Enough about men," she said. "Now let's get back to talking about flowers for your big day."

Ellis unlocked his front door, trudged inside, kicked the door closed behind him and dropped into the nearest chair. He'd thrown himself into work today, hoping that exhaustion would help him to sleep better than he had over the past week. These past few days had been miserable. He'd woken each morning, his heart aching with loneliness. He missed Tiffany more than he had ever missed anyone. He yearned to hear her sweet voice saying his name. The way she pronounced *Ellis* was different from the way that every other person said it. Just hearing his name on her lips awakened emotions that had previously lain dormant. He'd wanted to explore them further but, sadly, she'd been uninterested.

Their last conversation played in his mind. Once

more, he asked himself whether he could have done something differently. What if instead of simply kissing her goodbye, he'd gone inside with her to talk? What if?

He pulled off his boots and set them on the floor. Why did he keep doing this to himself? Rehashing everything wasn't going to change anything. It only served to make him miserable. He'd considered calling her to talk, but he realized the futility of doing that. What exactly would they say? She'd been perfectly clear about what she wanted for her life and what she didn't. Love wasn't something that you could argue about. You couldn't persuade someone to care about you. Either they did or they didn't. Sadly for him, Tiffany didn't.

No, that wasn't entirely accurate. He believed that she did care about him. Not as deeply as he had come to care about her, but it was obvious that she felt something for him. Given time, that feeling could have grown. But only if she nurtured it, which she wouldn't. It didn't make sense for him to allow his feelings for her to grow under these circumstances. And if he was around her, that was exactly what would happen. So the best thing to do, the wiser thing to do, was to stay away from her.

It wasn't as if Tiffany was the only woman in town. He knew plenty of nice women that he could spend time with. Women who actually wanted to be with him. He scrolled through the contacts in his phone, looking at the long list of eligible women. Yet as he considered which one to call, he realized that he didn't want to go out with any of them. Tiffany had wormed her way into his heart and she was the only woman he wanted to be with. Dating another woman would be like cheating on

Tiffany—something he could never do. Not only that, it wouldn't be fair to go out with one woman when his mind and heart were with another.

So just where did that leave him? He couldn't spend the rest of his life pining away for someone who didn't want him. That would be a waste of the gift of life. He might not know what his next step was going to be, but he knew that it wasn't that. And he wasn't going to call Tiffany like some crazed stalker ex-boyfriend who couldn't take "I'm not interested" for an answer. He rubbed his eyes. He knew he wasn't making sense. It was impossible to think clearly when he was this tired. Groaning, he pushed to his feet and stumbled into the bathroom for a long soak in his tub. The hot water did little to clear the mess in his mind, but the aches in his body faded away. If only the pain in his heart could be soothed as easily.

The next day was a scheduled off day for him, so he saddled Smokey and went for a ride. Though he didn't have a destination in mind, he wasn't surprised when he ended up at the watering hole. Memories of being there with Tiffany immediately flashed though his mind. He could practically see her walking around the pond, her round hips swaying sexily with each step she took. He sat on the boulder and recalled sitting there beside her, her sweet scent wafting around him. His ears rang with the echo of her laughter. *Great.* Just what he didn't need. Though she was alive and well, Tiffany was haunting him. There had to be a way to exorcise her from his brain. And if that worked, he might be able to get her out of his heart.

Since there was no peace to be found here, Ellis hopped back on Smokey, then headed back for the stable. He was grooming the horse when his brothers walked in together.

"Hey," Ellis said, looking up briefly before returning his attention to Smokey. He gave the stallion one last brush and led him into his stall. When he reached the front of the stable, his brothers were still standing there. "What's up?"

"That's what we want to know," Tristan said.

"What do you mean?" Ellis wiped off his saddle with a damp cloth to remove all traces of sweat and residue. Once it was clean, he hung it on the rack.

His brothers exchanged glances, not saying a word until he was done. That didn't bode well. He shook his head. He might as well get this over with.

"You haven't been yourself these past couple of days," Aaron said. "What gives?"

"If I'm not me, then who am I? And why do these clothes fit so well?"

Shane shook his head. "I knew you wouldn't take this seriously."

"There's no sense trying to deny there's a problem," Aaron said. "We're your brothers. We're on your side."

"We only want the best for you," Tristan added.

They all looked so sincere and sounded so concerned that the joking reply Ellis was going to make died on his lips. Instead he sighed and headed out the door, his brothers right behind him. He didn't want to go to the main house—his parents were there and some conversations were for brothers only—so he walked over to the corral. He hooked his foot on the lower rail and leaned on the top one, staring at the horses. He noted absently that his brothers did the same.

"It's Tiffany." Ellis hadn't planned to just blurt it out like that. In fact, he hadn't intended to mention any of this to his brothers. But it was too late to call the words back.

"What about her?" Shane asked.

"Don't tell me she broke up with you," Tristan said, a wide grin on his face. When Ellis only stared, Tristan's smile faded.

"Way to go," Aaron said, poking his brother in the side. The nudge could have been harder in Ellis's estimation, but that was pure meanness on his part.

"Oh, no. Sorry. I was just kidding," Tristan said quickly. "She really broke up with you?"

"We weren't really together to begin with," Ellis said, as much to himself as his brothers. But though that might technically be true, it did little to salve his heartache. The fact that they were only having a fling was a mere technicality. He had been all in.

"Tell that to somebody who'll believe it," Shane said.

Sighing, Ellis turned and leaned his back against the fence, then lifted his face to the sky. The sun was shining brightly. A puffy cloud floated across the otherwise blue sky. A gentle breeze blew, kicking up a small cloud of dirt around his feet. It was a perfect day. Somehow that only made things worse. It would be better if it were cold and rainy, matching his dreary mood. Then if he cried, he could pretend that the tears were raindrops. Not that he planned to cry. But then, he hadn't planned to fall in love with a woman who could walk away from him without looking back either.

"We weren't together," he repeated. "When we met, Tiffany made it clear that she wasn't looking for a serious relationship. And that was fine with me because I wasn't either."

"But you are now?" Aaron asked, his voice incredulous. And slightly horrified.

"I didn't say that."

"You don't have to pretend with us," Tristan said.

"I'm not pretending." Ellis blew out a long breath. "In the beginning, I wasn't looking for anything permanent. You know that. I've always preferred to be with women who only wanted a good time. Women who didn't want a commitment because I didn't want one either."

"That sounds like a perfect plan to me. What changed?" Aaron asked.

"I'm not sure. I guess the more time I spent with Tiffany, the more time I wanted to spend with her. And the more we were together, the more I came to care about her. Before I knew it, she had become important to me. So important that I couldn't imagine living life without her. No, that's not right. I *can* imagine living without her. I just don't want to. But I don't have a choice." Ellis looked at his brothers. He knew that Shane would understand how he felt. Shane was going to marry Remi one day. He would be gutted if she walked away from him. But he wasn't sure if his younger brothers understood. Tristan and Aaron were happily enjoying their single status. The same as Ellis had been before Tiffany waltzed into his life with her laughter and flowers.

"So what went wrong? Did you guys have a fight or something?" Tristan asked.

"I wish it was something like that. Everything was fine." Until he started talking about marriage. Then Tiffany had headed for the hills, leaving him in her dust. Ellis rubbed the spot in between his eyes, wishing he could rub away the pain. He'd hoped that talking about what went wrong with Tiffany would make him feel better. Instead, it only gave him a headache.

"How about you get her some flowers? Women can't resist flowers," Aaron said.

"What are you? The woman whisperer?" Tristan asked.

Despite himself, Ellis laughed. Tristan had a way with words. "Tiffany is a florist. She's surrounded by flowers all day long."

But she had liked the flowers and painted pot he'd given her at Dinosaur Days. And she had said she would have liked getting a bouquet from time to time. Not that it mattered now.

"So you know that she loves flowers," Aaron said, then turned to Tristan. "And yes, I am the woman whisperer. Thanks for the new title."

"Whether or not she likes flowers is immaterial," Shane said. "That's not going to make her change her mind about having a serious relationship with Ellis."

"Is that the goal?" Tristan asked. "I don't see the point of chasing a woman and trying to convince her to love you. Either she does or she doesn't. In your case…"

"Way to bring him down even lower," Aaron said, punching Tristan in the shoulder.

"Why lie?" Tristan asked, punching Aaron back. If this kept up, they'd be wrestling in the dirt before long.

"Knock it off, you two," Shane said. "We're supposed to be coming up with constructive ideas here."

Ellis only shook his head. "Is that what you're supposed to be doing?"

"Yes. I guess we're not doing such a good job of coming up with an answer if you can't tell," Shane said.

"I'm not sure there's an answer."

"Of course there is," Tristan said. "Every problem has at least one solution."

"Really?" Ellis said. "Then tell me how to get Tiffany to change her mind about our relationship."

"I need more facts first. What did she say? All you've told us is that she doesn't want to be with you. There has to be a reason."

"All I know is that she isn't a big fan of Tenacity. It's a little too rustic for her. And there isn't as much to do here as there is in Bronco. Not to mention her business. She worked hard to make it a success. That definitely ties her to Bronco."

"Well, as much as I hate to admit it, she's not wrong," Tristan replied. "Tenacity and Bronco are worlds apart. And if she is looking for a place on par with her town, she won't find it here."

"*Now*," Ellis said. "She won't find it now. But once the dig gets going, the town will have a whole lot more money. We'll be able to build it up. And businesses will come. She could open another florist shop here."

"That sounds good in theory," Aaron said, frowning. "But even if things work out the way you hope, which is doubtful because there's always a hitch, we're talking about years. Do you expect her to hang around that long?"

"It'll take years to complete the project, sure. But improvements will be made over time. Once Tiffany sees the changes, she'll change her mind about Tenacity," Ellis said confidently.

"What if it isn't just that?" Aaron asked.

"Meaning what?" Ellis asked.

"What if it's you?" Aaron said.

"Aaron," Shane said, warning in his tone.

"Or what if she really does prefer to be single right now?" Aaron persisted stubbornly. "Since that's what I want, I completely understand. To be honest, there's nothing a woman could say to make me change my mind."

Ellis shook his head. "I can't think that way. There has to be something I can do. I just haven't thought of it yet."

His brothers exchanged glances. Shane spread out his arms. "I got nothing."

Ellis looked at Tristan and Aaron. "Don't you two have anything to say?"

"Keep hope alive," Tristan said.

"Uh. Ditto," Aaron added before he, Shane and Tristan walked away.

"Thanks for nothing," Ellis called to his brothers' retreating backs. But then, what did he expect? His brothers were just as confused as he was. None of them understood how a woman thought. If he wanted to know that, there was only one thing to do.

He was going to have to ask Michelle.

Chapter Eleven

"Argh," Tiffany muttered at the knock on her door, setting her half-eaten bowl of chocolate chip ice cream on the table. She paused the movie she was pretending to watch, then put the remote on the table between the stack of chocolate bars and a can of soda. She should probably grab a bag of chips from the pantry while she was up, just in case she got a yearning for salt. She swiped at a drop of ice cream on her T-shirt, shrugged indifferently, then headed to the door. Tiffany looked through the peephole and blew out a breath. Brittany and Stephanie. Any other time she would be happy to see her sisters, but not tonight. Tonight she just wanted to pig out on junk food and wallow.

"We know you're in there," Brittany called through the closed door. "Knocking was simply a courtesy."

"Yeah," Stephanie added. "We have keys and we aren't afraid to use them."

Grumbling about nosy sisters, Tiffany unlocked the door and stepped aside to let them in.

Stephanie took a look around and then, shaking her head, she dropped into the nearest chair. "This is worse than I imagined."

"What is?" Tiffany asked.

"You. The way you're mourning the end of your relationship," Stephanie said.

"We're just in time," Brittany added, sitting in the place on the couch that Tiffany had just vacated.

"In time for what?" Tiffany asked warily. She was still standing by the door and could make a break for it if necessary.

"This is an intervention," Brittany said.

"A what?" She had to have heard wrong.

"An intervention," Brittany repeated.

"Aren't those for addicts?"

"They're for anyone who is suffering and in need of help," Stephanie said. "And it is clear to us that you need help."

"I'm fine," Tiffany said. She closed the door and crossed the room. Picking up her bowl of ice cream, she scooped up a heaping spoonful and ate it. She was definitely going to need a big dose of sugar to get through this nonsense.

"Obviously," Brittany said, rolling her eyes. She gestured at Tiffany's snacks. "Are you preparing to enter an eating contest?"

"Just for that remark, I won't be offering you anything."

"Since when do we stand on formality?" As if to prove that point, Brittany picked up a chocolate bar, unwrapped it and took a bite. Stephanie did the same.

"Since the two of you decided that I needed an intervention."

"You skipped out on girls' night out," Stephanie said

as if that explained her and Brittany's behavior. "You never do that."

"Maybe I decided I preferred my own company. Did you ever think of that?"

"No," Stephanie said. "Try again."

"I needed some time alone."

"Time alone to do what?" Stephanie asked. "Give yourself a bellyache? Trust me, the pain in your stomach won't make the pain in your heart any more bearable."

Tiffany pursed her lips and folded her arms over her chest. "I don't know what you're talking about."

"I'm talking about Ellis," Stephanie said gently. "I saw the way you were when the two of you were together. You were positively glowing. I've never seen you happier."

"I'm a little bit miffed that I didn't get to meet him," Brittany said. "But I'll meet him when the two of you get back together."

"We aren't going to get back together," Tiffany said quickly. Saying the words out loud was painful and suddenly she felt as if a dagger pierced her heart.

"Why not?" Stephanie asked, taking another bite of her candy bar.

"I'm not looking for a permanent relationship. When Ellis told me he wanted to get serious, I reminded him of that."

"Wait a minute. He wanted to get serious?" Stephanie asked.

"Didn't I just say that?" Tiffany snapped. She wasn't usually this short-tempered, but her nerves were a bit frayed right now. She knew she wasn't fit to be around people, which was why she'd skipped tonight.

"And?" Stephanie prompted.

"And nothing."

"It sounds like something to me," Brittany said.

"It's not. We went on a date. When it ended, Ellis brought me home. He hasn't called me since."

"Did you call him?"

"No." She'd chased after her ex, which had been a horrible mistake. She wouldn't chase after Ellis.

"Why not?" Stephanie asked.

Tiffany blew out a breath. "Isn't it obvious?"

Brittany and Stephanie exchanged glances. Then Stephanie spoke. "Not to us."

"There are so many reasons."

"Give us one," Stephanie said.

"Each," Brittany added.

Tiffany flung out her arms. "He hasn't called me. And I understand why he hasn't. He wants more than I can give him."

"What makes you think that you can't give him what he wants?" Brittany asked.

"Because I don't want to. That should be reason enough."

"You need to stop being so scared of getting hurt," Stephanie said.

"That's easy for you to say. You weren't engaged to a cheating weasel."

"Surely you don't think you're the only woman who has trusted the wrong man." Brittany said. "It has happened to more women than you know. And it was never the woman's fault. And it certainly wasn't yours."

Remi had said something along those same lines. Tiffany had listened, but had she really heard?

"But that doesn't mean that every man is a liar," Stephanie added. "There are still some good ones around."

"I know," Tiffany said. "But it makes it hard to trust."

"Hard to trust him or yourself?" Brittany asked.

"Both."

"So you don't trust Ellis?" Stephanie asked.

"I didn't say that. I do trust him. I know he is just as honest and good as he seems."

"Then if you trust him, that means that you've made a good decision," Brittany said.

"And that means you can trust yourself, too." Stephanie said, a satisfied look on her face.

Tiffany gave those statements due consideration, then nodded slowly. "But it's too late now. Ellis doesn't want anything to do with me. Otherwise he would have reached out."

"Or maybe he loves you and he's doing the same thing you were doing. He's protecting his heart from further pain. After all, you did reject him and everything he was offering."

Love? There was suddenly a buzzing sound in her head and Tiffany found it hard to think straight. That one word kept reverberating in her head. *Love.* Was it possible that Ellis loved her? He hadn't said that. At least not in those words. But he had said that his feelings for her had grown. Did she want him to love her?

The only reason she would was if she loved him, too. Only a self-centered woman would go around collecting hearts. She had her flaws, but being self-centered wasn't one of them. So, she supposed she did love him. Surprisingly, the idea didn't horrify her. Nor was she scared. In fact, she liked the idea.

"I didn't think of it that way," Tiffany said softly.

"Maybe you should," Stephanie said.

"And maybe you should get some more snacks to share with your sisters," Brittany said. "Girls' night out just became girls' night in."

"So are you going to tell me why you wanted to come here?" Michelle asked, looking around the Grizzly Bar. "I mean, we both live and work on the same ranch. We could have talked there and saved gas."

Ellis shook his head. He'd known that his sister wouldn't make this easy for him. That would be against her nature. But he hadn't expected the questions to start before they'd even shot one game of pool. "I thought you would appreciate a change of scenery. As you pointed out, we live and work in the same place. Surely you get tired of seeing the same things day after day."

Michelle laughed. "Not really. But we can do things your way. Just as long as you don't expect me to go easy on you. And no whining when I take your money."

"You're awfully confident for someone who has never beaten me in a game of pool before. But I suppose there has to be a first time."

What Michelle lacked in skill she made up for in the ability to talk trash. "I was just letting you get overconfident." She rubbed her hands together. "Now I have you right where I want you."

"Ooh, I'm so scared." Ellis pretended to shiver and they both laughed.

Michelle shot, breaking the balls and sinking the orange striped one. "I got stripes."

Ellis nodded. "Okay."

She pushed Ellis out the way, then lined up her next shot. And missed. She moved away from the table so he could take his turn. Then she leaned on her stick and looked at him. "Seriously, what did you want to talk about?"

He sighed. The time for beating around the bush had clearly come and gone. "It's Tiffany."

Michelle smiled. "I liked her."

"So did I."

"*Did.* Past tense. That doesn't sound good."

"No." He put down his cue and stepped away from the table.

"A forfeit counts as a loss," Michelle said.

Ellis shrugged. "I guess I'll have to start another streak next time."

"Oh, you must really be hurting." Michelle stepped closer, her eyes filled with sympathy. "How can I help?"

"Let's sit down and talk."

They picked up their drinks and returned to their table. Ellis leaned back in his chair and looked at his sister. "Tell me… What do women want?"

"For men to recognize that we are not a monolith," Michelle said, her voice as dry as dust.

"Michelle, please."

"Every woman wants something different." She took a sip of her cola, then looked into his eyes, obviously seeing way too much. "But you don't want to know about every woman. You want to know about Tiffany."

"Yeah."

"How would I know what she wants? I only met her once. We talked for a few minutes. You were there and heard everything that was said."

He shook his head. Why couldn't Michelle show mercy for once in her life? "You're a woman."

"Thanks for noticing."

"Michelle." His voice was both a warning and a plea. The fact that he didn't know how to react only emphasized his desperation.

"What did she say she wants?"

"Not a relationship. She wants to be friends." His lips twisted at the last word.

"Really? That's not the impression I got."

"It isn't?" Ellis heard the hope in his voice but he didn't try to suppress it. He would hold on to any scrap of hope he could find.

"No."

"Then why did she end things with me?"

"I have no idea. What happened?"

Ellis sighed and picked at the label of his beer bottle. "I told her that my feelings for her had changed and that I wanted something more than a fling. Something permanent."

"That doesn't sound like a reason to end things. Something else must have happened. Something you haven't told me." Michelle shook her head slowly. "I can't help you if you hide things from me."

"The whole time we were seeing each other, she kept harping on our differences. You know, I'm country and she's city. She loves Bronco and Tenacity can't hold a candle to it. She has a business in Bronco and doesn't think a florist shop will thrive in Tenacity."

"I don't think she's as hung up on zip codes as she's led you to believe. That sounds like an excuse. I think that there's something else driving her."

"What?"

"I have no idea. But instead of asking me, why don't you ask her? Only she knows her true reasons." Michelle tilted her head. "When is the last time that you talked to her?"

"The day we went riding. That was when I told her I wanted more and she shut me down."

Michelle frowned. "She hurt your feelings so you picked up your bat and ball and went home."

"That's not what I intended. I was trying to respect her feelings. Not pressure her into a relationship she didn't want." He thought about it. "But maybe you're right. It's possible that I walked away because I was hurt. I care about her. A lot. If friendship is all that she can give right now, I'll try to accept that. But I really hope that at some point she'll want something more."

"Talk to her. Don't try to convince her to do anything. Just listen. If you give her some space, I believe she'll tell you why she's so opposed to relationships. Then you'll know what to do next. But if there is no underlying reason, you're going to have to respect her decision. Either way, you won't know if you don't talk to her."

"You're right. I don't know why I didn't think of it."

"You're too close to the situation. And you know that you could end up hurt again. Nobody likes pain so it's reasonable for you to do what you can to avoid it."

He nodded.

Michelle looked into his eyes and spoke softly. "But if you avoid pain, you might end up avoiding happiness, too. You don't want to do that."

"No, I don't." He breathed out a long breath. "Thanks."

"Sure." Michelle stood. "But let's get back to our game. I don't want my first victory over you to be the result of a forfeiture. I want to earn my bragging rights."

Ellis nodded. He was so happy now that he actually considered going easy on her.

They played two games and Ellis won both of them easily. They returned their sticks to the rack.

"I let you win," Michelle said as they walked back to his truck.

"Is that right?" Ellis asked, pulling into the street and heading back to the ranch.

"Yep. But next time, I'm not going to have mercy on you."

Ellis laughed. When they got back to the ranch, Ellis dropped Michelle at her house and then drove the short distance to his.

Though it was late, he felt energized for the first time in a week. He knew what he was going to do. He had put all of his brain power into his mayoral campaign.

He hadn't won, but he'd left it all out there. The fact that he had come up short didn't change that fact.

The campaign to win Tiffany's love was more important than being mayor had ever been. This was going to take more than his brain. He was going to have to risk it all by opening his heart again.

His grandmother and the children at the Little Cowpokes Daycare would be planting flowers in the garden on Monday. Tiffany had promised to help. She was as good as her word so he knew that she would be there. If he was going to win her heart, he was going to have to prove to her that he was as good as his.

Chapter Twelve

"You can do this," Tiffany murmured to herself early Monday morning. "Remember, you are magnificent."

Too bad she didn't feel magnificent. She hadn't felt that way since that day on the ranch.

She'd spent the past ten minutes parked in front of the Little Cowpokes Daycare Center. Two women had glanced at the Blossom Truck as they'd exited the building, walked back to their cars and driven away. A man had dropped off a little boy before coming up to her window and asking if she needed help. She did need help, but since she doubted he had anything to repair her broken heart, she assured him she was fine.

She knew the possibility of running into Ellis was slim. After all, there was no reason for him to be here. And since they hadn't talked to each other in over a week, she didn't think he'd seek her out today. Even so, she vacillated between hoping to see him and dreading the possibility. She didn't know which would be worse. Either way, her heart wouldn't get away unscathed. But driving out of Tenacity now wasn't an option—she'd made a promise that she intended to keep—and she couldn't continue sitting in her Blossom Truck either.

Inhaling deeply, Tiffany grabbed her shopping bags of supplies, got out of her vehicle and walked up to the daycare. The sounds of singing came from the back of the building so she made a detour. She peered over the white picket fence. The preschoolers were sitting in small chairs in a semicircle. Angela was leading them in a song about spring. When the last strains of the melody faded away, Tiffany applauded.

Angela looked over at her and smiled. She hurried across the yard and opened the gate. "You're right on time."

"I wish I had been a minute or two earlier so I could have heard more of the song."

"We're practicing for Parents' Day at the end of May. Our performance is always a big hit. But this garden is going to be a big hit, too."

"I have a few tools for the kids. I saw these cute little hand shovels in bright colors and I couldn't resist."

"You didn't have to do that."

Tiffany shrugged. "I know, but I think it will help the kids enjoy gardening all summer. As a florist, I have a vested interest in awakening their love of flowers. I look at it as an investment in the future."

Angela laughed. "I haven't met a kid yet who didn't enjoy digging in the dirt."

"I see your point. But now they'll be digging with a purpose. And with pretty tools."

"You seem to understand the little ones quite well."

"My two sisters have young children so I've gotten a lot of experience with the younger set."

"That might explain part of it, but I think you're a

natural." Angela smiled at her. "You'll make a great mother one day."

Tiffany didn't know what to say to that. Fortunately, Angela didn't seem to want a response. Instead, she helped Tiffany carry the supplies to the site of the planned garden. Tiffany looked around. An impressive amount of work had been done since she'd last been here. There were two rectangular raised beds that had been filled with soil. Small containers of pansies were in neat rows beside one of the beds. Petunias were beside the other.

"You've done a lot already. I was prepared for a lot of digging." Tiffany pointed to her faded jeans and old shirt.

"The parents did most of the work. Of course, it doesn't hurt to have strong grandsons who did the rest. But that kind of support is expected. Tenacity is a place where people help each other. All I had to do was spread the word about what I needed and people stepped up. A few farmers donated the plants."

Ellis had told her on more than one occasion how great the people of Tenacity were. Had she let the lack of spas and fancy boutiques make her forget that it was the citizens who made a town? You could paint a building, pave the streets and plant flowers to make everything pretty. But no amount of cosmetics could change what was in someone's heart. In this case, the goodness in the people's hearts more than made up for the town's appearance. Knowing that she'd made a similar mistake about Ellis broke her heart. She'd misjudged him, too. She knew that he was nothing at all like her ex.

Ellis was good to the core of his being. If she ever got a second chance with him, she wasn't going to blow it.

But this wasn't the place or time to think about her personal problems. There were currently two dozen children waiting to get the show on the road. Angela and Tiffany passed out the garden trowels, letting the children choose the color they wanted. Several of the kids danced, their little bodies wiggling in excitement. Two kids placed their trowels on their heads, wearing them like crowns while two others pretended to sword fight. All in all, it was a wonderful, if slightly chaotic, scene.

Once every child had a tool Angela looked at Tiffany. "This is your show."

"Oh. I thought I was just helping."

"You are helping. You're a florist so I'm sure you know some things about plants and gardening that I don't. I plan on learning from you."

Tiffany hadn't expected to be in charge, but there was no time to object. Not that it would do any good. Angela had already moved to stand behind the students who were getting even antsier. Inhaling deeply, Tiffany picked up a plastic green container, holding it high so all of the kids could see it. "This is a pansy plant. Right now it lives in this little pot. It fits now because it's little, too. But it wants to get bigger, so we're going to give it a new home in this big planter. That way it can grow and produce beautiful flowers."

A little boy patted Tiffany's knee. "I have a house. It's way bigger than this. The flowers can live with me."

"That's nice of you to offer. But the pansy and petunias needs dirt."

"My mom says my room is dirty. Then she makes me clean it all the time. I don't like cleaning up. If I had a plant, maybe I could leave it dirty," he said seriously.

Tiffany managed to suppress a laugh, but she couldn't hold back her smile. "The plant needs a different kind of dirt to grow. It needs soil. And it will be happier here in the garden."

"If you say so," the little boy said, his tone making it very clear that he doubted Tiffany's wisdom.

"I do."

Two teachers helped Tiffany and Angela organize the kids around the first bed. Once the kids had put on tiny garden gloves and plastic smocks that would help them stay relatively clean, Tiffany showed them how to use the trowel to dig a small hole in the dirt. Then the adults took a step back and let the children work. As expected, there was dirt everywhere in under a minute, including on Tiffany. But she didn't mind. When the kids were finished digging, Tiffany helped them gently remove their plants from the pots and place them into the holes.

The children asked all kinds of questions as they worked and Tiffany answered them all, trying to use words and explanations the children would understand. She wanted them to feel proud of themselves when they looked at the garden so she was careful not to provide too much assistance. If their plants were a little crooked, that was fine. They would still grow into beautiful flowers.

The little ones' enthusiasm was contagious and Tiffany found herself smiling more than she had since she and Ellis had broken up. It was impossible to be sad when she was surrounded by so much joy.

As she interacted with the kids, Tiffany imagined what it would be like to have children of her own to love. Children that she could have shared with Ellis. He was so gentle and kind. The best man she'd ever met. Without a doubt, he would be a great father. And she'd walked away from him. Everything was ruined and she couldn't see a way to clean up the mess she'd made. Thinking of the way she'd dismissed Ellis's feelings made her heart ache. He'd been offering love and a future, and all she'd had to say was yes. Instead she'd let her fear chase him away. Now she was heartbroken and alone, and she had no one to blame but herself.

Her vision blurred as her eyes filled with tears and she hastily brushed them away. This was no time for a pity party. She forced herself to concentrate on the task at hand. Once the pansies were planted, the kids moved to the other flower bed and repeated the process. This time they sang as they worked.

Once the flowers were planted, some a tad too deep, the kids stood back, happy smiles on their faces. Angela took off her garden gloves and then held a finger up to her lips. In a few moments the children settled down. Tiffany expected Angela to make a wrap-up speech, congratulating the students on a job well done. Instead, the older woman looked over Tiffany's shoulder and smiled broadly.

Before Tiffany could turn to see what had drawn Angela's attention, a flowerpot filled with yellow tulips, purple hyacinths and pink roses appeared in front of her. Her three favorite flowers. Her gaze moved from the flowers to the man holding them.

Ellis.

Tiffany was vaguely aware of Angela and the other teachers leading the children inside the building, leaving Tiffany and Ellis alone. Words failed her as she stared into the beloved face of the man she'd missed so desperately these long, lonely days. Her heart began to pound and despite the fact that she didn't want to get ahead of herself, hope began to sprout inside of her.

"Do you have a minute?" Ellis asked, his voice soft. Gentle as always. "I hoped that we could talk."

Tiffany nodded. "Yes. I'm finished here."

Ellis took a look around and then smiled at her. "Thanks for helping my grandmother with the garden. I could tell that the kids had a great time."

"I did, too." Tiffany paused. "How long were you watching?"

"Awhile. You were great with the kids. You really connected with them."

Tiffany recalled how she'd once imagined teaching her kids about gardening. At the time, the dream seemed unreachable. Now the idea of having kids with Ellis, though still not near, didn't seem quite as far away. A happy melody began to play in her heart as joy began to bloom.

"I brought these flowers as part of my apology," Ellis said, offering them to her.

"What do you need to apologize for? You didn't do anything wrong."

Maybe Ellis wasn't here to try to rekindle their relationship. Maybe he just wanted to end things on good terms. The hope that had sprung up inside her began to wither. The song in her heart was silenced.

"Yes, I did. I acted like a spoiled brat just because I didn't get my way. I shouldn't have ghosted you like that. I'm ashamed for behaving so childishly."

"That goes both ways. I didn't reach out to you either."

"True. But when I didn't get the reaction that I expected to get—that I *hoped* to get—I acted like a jerk. And really, I had no reason to be disappointed by your answer. You'd made it clear from the very beginning that you didn't want anything other than a fling with me. And I agreed. Just because I started to want more didn't give me the right to be upset when you wanted to stick to the original plan. And for that, you deserve an apology."

"Well, since we're being honest now, I need to tell you something. My…reaction…had nothing to do with you. It was all about me. And my past." She took a deep breath and forced herself to continue. "I should have told you the truth, but I was embarrassed. To be honest, I'm still embarrassed. But I'm not going to let it stop me from talking to you."

Ellis led her to the bench at the edge of the yard and brushed off dirt that had landed there. Once they were seated, he removed her soiled garden gloves and took her hands in his, as if trying to infuse her with strength. Tiffany looked into his eyes. The kindness and compassion she saw there made her brave. She should have known that Ellis would never judge her. More than that, she should have trusted her instincts when they told her that he was a good man. The best man. But she'd let her fear rule. Thankfully, she'd been given a second chance.

"Can you tell me about it now?" His voice was gentle. Just like him.

Tiffany swallowed and then gave a tight, humorless smile. "It's an old and not unfamiliar story. I was engaged to a man who was seeing someone else. He was also…engaged…to her."

She paused and took a deep breath. She didn't want to see the expression on Ellis's face, so she stared at her hands. "Neither of us knew about the other. I never even suspected that he was unfaithful. I believed the excuses he gave me for why he couldn't spend time with me. I even made up explanations of my own to account for his absences. Looking back, it all seems so ridiculous. I feel so stupid."

"You shouldn't. You didn't do anything wrong. You were honest and had an open heart. You believed because you were faithful and expected the person you were in love with to be faithful, too. And that's the way it's supposed to be. You should be able to trust the person who claims to love you. The fact that he was untrustworthy is on him, not you. You aren't to blame for his deceit. Nor were you stupid. If anyone was stupid, it was him. He should have treasured you."

"I've finally started to believe that. But that didn't make trusting you any easier."

"Because you think that all men are cheaters and liars?" He sounded sad. Defeated even.

"*Thought.* I no longer think that way thanks to you."

He flashed the smile that she had grown to love. "I'm glad that I could help."

"But that's not the only reason I walked away from you. I lost confidence in myself and my judgment. You were honest and open with me. But..."

"But you couldn't trust me."

"I couldn't trust *myself.* I didn't want to lead myself down the primrose path again. I let a man fool me once. I wasn't going to let another one do it again, no matter how charming you were and how much fun we had together. No matter how honest you seemed. I couldn't let myself hope for something real. I figured if I put a limit on our relationship, a limit on my feelings, I couldn't get hurt again."

"And then I went and started talking about marriage of all things." He shook his head, a pained expression marring his handsome face. "I can see how that would make you want to keep your distance from me. I shouldn't have rushed you to tell me how you felt. If anything, I should have kept quiet and given your feelings a chance to grow. But I just blurted it out and demanded a response. And in the end, I put pressure on you and chased you away."

"That's not what made me cautious," Tiffany admitted. "It's the fact that what you were offering sounded so good. Too good. If I didn't run away I'd have to face the truth of my feelings. I had to admit that I was falling in love with you, too. And that whole idea was terrifying."

Ellis's heart skipped a beat and then began to race. Unable to believe it, he looked at Tiffany. He needed to hear that again. "Did you just say that you love me?"

She nodded and gave him a shy smile. “It sounded like that to me.”

He leaned back against the bench. “I dare you to say it again.”

“Funny, I was just about to dare you to say it to me. After all, it has been a while. For all I know, you’ve changed your mind.”

That last bit revealed quite a bit about Tiffany’s fears. She’d been hurt so badly in the past that a part of her must have believed he could stop loving her. Never. She was a part of his heart. Ellis sat up straight and stared into Tiffany’s eyes. He needed her to see the sincerity in his and put her doubts to rest once and for all. “I don’t need a dare in order to tell you that I love you. I love you, Tiffany Brandt. More than anything in the world. And I always will. You can trust that.”

Tiffany’s smile widened. “I love you, too.”

He nodded. “It sounds just as good the second time around.”

“So what happens now?”

“I suppose we should pick up where we left off.” He shook his head ruefully. “I know I have a tendency to go fast, but I’m willing to take baby steps if that’s what it takes to make you feel comfortable. I know it will take effort on both of our parts, but we can make the long-distance thing work for as long as necessary. That way I can keep working on the ranch and you can work at your shop. And we can decide what to do in the future when that time arrives.”

“I like that plan. And I like the way things were progressing between us. I enjoyed our dates. Especially the time we spent together after dinner at DJ's Deluxe. And I definitely think we should repeat that soon." She gave him a sexy look that made the blood pulse in his veins. "But there is one thing I definitely want to do."

Tiffany smiled and leaned against Ellis's side. He wrapped his arm around her, pulling her closer. He inhaled her familiar sweet scent. He would do whatever made her happy. "What's that? Take in a Broadway show? Visit Chicago to see their dinosaur?"

"Both of those things sound good and they're definitely on the list, but that's not what I was thinking about."

"Then what?"

"I would like to have Easter dinner with your family."

Ellis smiled. "My parents would love that."

"How would you feel?"

"I would be thrilled and honored to have you by my side."

Tiffany picked up the flowerpot and touched one of the tulips. "I really love those flowers. You remembered that I said these are my favorite."

"I remember everything that you ever told me," he said quietly.

"You do?" Her head swung around as she turned to look at him.

"Of course. You're important to me. So if it matters to you, it matters to me."

Tiffany turned the flowerpot. He'd painted it just like the one he'd made at the Dinosaur Days event. He watched, waiting as she continued turning the pot.

When she noticed what he'd inscribed, she gasped and looked back at him. "E ♥ T."

He gave her a crooked grin. "I wanted to be sure you got the message. I wrote it just in case you weren't ready to hear the words out loud yet."

Tears welled in Tiffany's eyes. "I love this flower pot and the message. And I'll never get tired of hearing you say the words."

"And I'll never get tired of saying them. I love you, Tiffany."

"I love you, too, Ellis."

Epilogue

"Thank you so much for inviting me to dinner," Tiffany said to Ellis's mother on Easter Sunday as she and the Corey family sat together in the comfortable family room. "It was delicious."

"We enjoyed having you," Patty said, smiling warmly.

"Although we're all still a bit perplexed about how someone as sweet and smart as you could fall for our lunkhead brother," Aaron said, laughing.

"Watch it," Ellis said, sending his brother a mock glare. That was the way the entire day had gone, with the siblings taking turns teasing each other. It had reminded Tiffany of Sunday dinners with her own family and she had instantly felt at home.

"I couldn't resist his charm and good looks," Tiffany said.

"Did you hear that?" Ellis said, flashing the grin that Tiffany had never been able to resist. "I'm charming and good-looking."

"She had to say that," Michelle said. "You're her ride home."

Tiffany looked at Ellis. “I would say that even if you weren’t my ride home.”

“Speaking of home…” Ellis rose and gave Tiffany’s hand a gentle squeeze. “We really need to get going.”

“So soon?” Patty asked.

“I’m afraid so,” Ellis said.

“Come back anytime,” Patty said, coming to give Tiffany a hug.

“Thanks. I will.”

After their goodbyes, Tiffany walked beside Ellis to his truck. Once they were inside, he turned to her. “Do you have a few minutes?”

“For you, I have a lifetime.” She fingered the diamond ring she was wearing on a chain around her neck. She wasn’t ready to wear it on her finger just yet, but soon.

Ellis smiled and drove toward his house. She’d been there a couple of times since they’d gotten back together. The decor was warm and masculine and reminded her of him. When they arrived, he opened the door and moved aside, allowing her to enter. Tiffany stepped in and gasped. There were pink rose petals scattered all over the front room. A large vase of pink roses was sitting in the middle of a wooden coffee table.

She turned to look at Ellis, who was smiling broadly. “Do you like it?”

“You know I do.” She shook her head. “But I don’t understand. Why did you do this?”

Ellis walked over and placed his hands on her waist, pulling her close to him. “Because I love you. And you like getting flowers.”

“I love you, too.” She slid her hands over his shoulders, rose on her tiptoes and kissed his lips. When he would have deepened the kiss, she stepped back. “There’s something I want to talk to you about.”

“That sounds ominous.”

“It’s not.” She took his hand and led him to the leather couch. “I’ve been thinking about my business. I’ve been considering the possibility of opening a Tiffany in Bloom location in Tenacity. I think I can negotiate a good rental agreement in one of the vacant buildings downtown. And I’ll get in on the ground floor of Tenacity’s renaissance.”

Tiffany had expected that to make him happy. Instead, his face turned serious. “I hope I haven’t made you feel pressured to do that.”

“You haven’t. I suppose being around you, and being around your family, has made me see Tenacity in a different light. I’ve come to care about the little town. It’s going to need more than dinosaur bones to make the town flourish. I think a little florist shop might be just what the doctor ordered.”

“I knew the town would win you over.”

“It has. Of course, opening a location here will have the added benefit of allowing me to spend more of my days and nights with you.”

“And just how do you intend to spend that time?” he asked, his voice seductive, his eyes dark with desire.

She took his hand and stood, heading for his bedroom. “Come on. I’ll show you.”

* * * * *